Each year the same thing

My whole life, I've always been an almost.

"Almost, Albie."

"Almost."

I was an almost in kindergarten when I asked if I could use markers at art time, instead of just crayons.

"Almost, Albie," the art teacher said. "Let's wait until your grip is a little stronger."

I was an almost in first grade when I wanted to walk our dog, Biscuit.

"Almost, Albie," my mom said. "He still tugs too hard for you."

I was an almost in second grade after I spent a whole weekend practicing my sounding-out words so I could move up to the red reading group.

"Almost, Albie," Miss Langhoff told me. "You have a tiny ways to go."

I was an almost in third grade too, when my poem wasn't picked for the wall for Parents' Night.

"Almost, Albie," Mr. Vidal said. "I almost put yours up. But there were so many to choose from."

By fourth grade, I was an almost every day.

"Almost, Albie."

That's what they tell me.

"Almost."

"Almost."

Always, *always* almost.

OTHER BOOKS YOU MAY ENJOY

ABSOLUTELY ALMOST

Lisa Graff

PUFFIN BOOKS

PUFFIN BOOKS
An imprint of Penguin Random House LLC
375 Hudson Street
New York, New York 10014

First published in the United States of America by Philomel Books,
an imprint of Penguin Group (USA) LLC, 2014
Published by Puffin Books, an imprint of Penguin Young Readers Group, 2015

THE LIBRARY OF CONGRESS HAS CATALOGED THE PHILOMEL BOOKS EDITION AS FOLLOWS:
Graff, Lisa.
Absolutely almost / Lisa Graff. pages cm
Summary: Ten-year-old Albie has never been the smartest, tallest, best at gym, greatest artist,
or most musical in his class, as his parents keep reminding him, but new nanny Calista helps
him uncover his strengths and take pride in himself.
ISBN: 978-0-399-16405-7 (hardcover)
[1. Self-esteem—Fiction. 2. Ability—Fiction. 3. Babysitters—Fiction.
4. Family life—New York (State)—New York—Fiction. 5. Schools—Fiction.
6. Racially mixed people—Fiction. 7. New York (N.Y.)—Fiction.]
I. Title. PZ7.G751577Abs 2014 [Fic]—dc23   2013023620

Puffin Books ISBN 978-0-14-750857-7

Printed in the United States of America

7 9 10 8 6

To Jill.

(Absolutely.)

rocks.

"Not everybody can be the rock at the top of the rock pile." That's what my Grandpa Park said to my mom once when they thought I was asleep, or just not listening, I don't know. But my ears work fine. "There have to be some rocks at the bottom, to support those at the top."

I sat in my bedroom, knocking the army men one by one off my windowsill. Dad said I was getting too old to play with them, so I didn't play, just knocked them over. *Plunk, plunk, plunk,* on the bedspread. But I did it quiet so no one would hear. *plunk . . . plunk.* For some reason, I felt heavy inside, listening to them talk out in the living room. Or maybe heavy on the outside, like something was pressing down on top of me, when really it was nothing but air. *plunk. plunk.*

If I listened real close, I could hear Grandpa Park's ice clicking in his glass when he lifted it to drink.

plunk.

It was quiet in the living room, no talking, only ice, for a long time. When I got to the last army man, I didn't set them up again right away. I stared at them on the bed, knocked over sideways or on their bellies. On some you could see the black marker where I'd marked their feet when I first learned to write my name. *A* for Albie.

It was quiet so long that I thought my mom must've gone to bed, and it was just Grandpa Park out there with his glass, drinking down till the ice melted like he usually did when he came to visit. But then Mom said something, so I knew she hadn't gone to bed after all. She said it real quiet, but I heard.

"Albie's not a rock," she said.

being friendly.

Tuesday evening was Chinese from the place on 61st Street, just like every Tuesday. When Bernard rang up from downstairs to let us know the delivery man was in the elevator, Mom gave me two twenties from her purse.

"Wait until he rings the buzzer, Albie," Mom told me. "And don't tip more than five."

"Okay," I told her, just as the bell rang.

It was my favorite delivery man, Wei. He always smiled big when he saw me.

"Albie!" he shouted, like he was surprised to see me

there, even though I answered the door every time. He lifted one of the food bags, like he was waving.

"Hi, Wei," I said, smiling back. "How much?"

"Twenty-seven sixty." He showed me the receipt stapled to one of the bags, because sometimes with numbers it was hard to understand what Wei was saying.

I took the bags and handed them to my mom, who put them on the table. They smelled greasy and meaty and delicious, like Tuesday evening. "Thanks," I told Wei, handing over the two twenties. "Can I get . . ." In my head I rounded up the change, like Mom and Dad do when they give tips in the cab. "Four dollars back?"

"Sure thing." Wei took a wad of bills out of his pocket and placed the twenties on the outside, then flicked past the tens and fives till he got to the ones, in the middle. He peeled off four for me.

"Here you go, Albie." Wei handed over the bills. "*Shee-shee.*" At least that's what it *sounded* like he said.

I raised an eyebrow at him.

"Thank you," he explained. "How do you say 'thank you' in Korean?"

I looked at Mom. Sometimes people think I know Korean, because I'm half, but I only know "hello" and a couple foods. Mom spoke it with her grandparents, but I don't think she likes to anymore.

Mom was busy setting the food out on plates, so she couldn't tell me how to say "thank you" to Wei in Korean.

"I'll tell you next time," I said.

He winked. "Bye, then!" he said.

"*Shee-shee!*" I answered, and I closed the door.

Dad snapped shut his laptop and got up from the couch as I handed Mom the change.

"Oh, Albie," Mom said, looking at the four dollars. "I said don't tip more than five."

I didn't, I started to say. *I just rounded up the change.* But before I could tell her that, Dad put a hand on my shoulder. "He was just being friendly. Weren't you, Albie?" He looked at Mom, still staring at the four ones. "It's just a few dollars."

That's when I started to get the feeling in my brain I sometimes got, when something that was clear before all of a sudden turned fuzzy. I sat down and Mom scooped some rice onto my plate, with kung pao and an egg roll.

Twenty-seven sixty. I put the number in my brain and tried to keep it there while I chewed my egg roll. Twenty-seven sixty. I'd started with forty dollars, and I gave Mom four. Over and over I tried to subtract the numbers, but I didn't want to do it on paper because I didn't want Mom and Dad to know I was subtracting, so it was hard. Every time I did it, I got a different number.

Fuzzy.

Fuzzier.

I gulped down the last of my egg roll.

"Everything okay, Albie?" Dad said, looking at me carefully.

"Yep," I told him. I picked up my fork and mixed the kung pao up with my rice, and decided that maybe I was being friendly after all.

letters
from school.

E-mails from school are never about good stuff. The teacher never writes to your parents to say things like "Albie's so wonderful to have in class! Just wanted to let you know!"

Or

"Albie always lets Rick Darby borrow his pencils, even though Rick barely ever gives them back!"

Or

"Today Albie picked Jessa Kwan first for his team in basketball, because Jessa usually gets picked last, and he felt bad!"

(My team lost in basketball that day.)

6

E-mails from school are always bad, but they try to hide it with big words that are hard to understand.

Potential.

Struggling.

Achievement gap.

Words that make my dad slam his fist on the table and call my teacher to shout about setting up a parent-teacher conference, and my mom to go out and buy fruit. When Mom comes back with strawberries, her face is always crystal clear. Not an almost-crying face at all.

I used to really like strawberries.

E-mails from school are always bad, and they're always about me. But *letters* from school—the kind that are written on real paper and sent in a real envelope, with a stamp and everything—those are even worse.

When the last letter came from Mountford Prep, my old school, Dad didn't yell at my teacher. Mom didn't go out and buy strawberries. They just sat at the table, blinking at me, their shoulders slumped like when our dog, Biscuit, ran away.

"What does it say?" I asked. It was open, in front of my dad across the table, but I couldn't see any of the words. Only the big red letters at the top of the page, spelling out the name of the school.

"It doesn't matter," Dad said. He looked mad, like his eyes were hurting him. He crunched up the letter and tossed it in the recycling.

"I think a new school will be good for you," Mom said.

• • •

It's my job to take the trash to the garbage chute every week, or whenever it's full. Recycling too. It's part of my chores. I get five dollars a week allowance.

That day, the letter day, I did my chores. But one tiny piece of recycling never made it down the chute. I smoothed out the letter from Mountford Prep, and folded it back along the creases, and put it in the bottom drawer of my dresser with my swim trunks.

I never read it. I didn't want to. But I didn't want to throw it out either. I don't know why.

Maybe P.S. 183 doesn't believe in sending home letters.

calista.

Mom waited two weeks for Dad to free up his schedule so he could help her pick the new nanny, but he kept being busy, so finally she picked by herself. The nanny came over on Tuesday to meet me.

"Hey, Albie," she said from the doorway. She waved one hand. The other was wrapped around a cup of takeout coffee from the bodega downstairs. I knew it was that bodega because I heard the owner, Hugo, say one time that they're the only ones for fourteen blocks who use the blue cups. "I'm Calista."

I didn't want to look up to meet her, but finally I did. It was better than the supplemental reading packets Mom had gotten for me, anyway.

She was short, but not too short for a girl, I guess. She was wearing jeans, even though it was too hot outside for jeans, and sandals, and a pink-and-orange plaid short-sleeve button-down shirt. Her hair was braided in two braids on either side of her head—not the regular kind of braids, but the complicated kind the girls do to each other during assemblies, the kind that start all the way above the ears and take forever. I wondered why she would wear her hair like that, because it made her look like a kid. Maybe that was why.

My mom walked to the kitchen and took a glass out of the cupboard. "Calista, would you like some water?" She started filling it before the new nanny even had a chance to answer. "Albie, don't be rude," Mom told me. "Say hello."

"I'm too old for a nanny," I said. Which was true, because I was ten.

"Albie!" Mom squawked. The ice tumbled out of the square in the fridge door and into the glass. "He's not normally like this," she told the nanny.

"That's all right," the girl said. But she didn't say it to my mom, she said it to me. She sat down in the chair next to me, still holding tight to her coffee, and smiled. "I'm not really a nanny," she said.

"More like a babysitter," Mom piped up from the kitchen.

I was too old for a babysitter too.

"We're just going to hang out together," the girl told me. "I'll pick you up from school. Maybe we'll go to the park a little bit, I'll help you with your homework."

"She can help you make flash cards to study," Mom said as the water poured in around the ice. I scrunched up my nose.

"And when your parents have to work late, we'll do dinner and play games," the girl went on. "Do you have Monopoly? I love Monopoly."

"That sounds like a babysitter," I told her.

My mom walked over and handed the girl the glass. It had little wet speckles of cold on the outside already. "Albie, you should show Calista your chess set. He has a gorgeous chess set, from Guatemala. Maybe you can practice so you can join the chess club at your new school. What do you think of that, hmm, Albie?"

I squinted at the girl.

"Just hanging out," she promised. She set the glass on the table, and my mom scooped it up to put a coaster underneath it.

I looked back down at my packet of supplemental materials. "I don't need to be picked up from school yet," I said. "There's still two weeks of summer."

"We thought Calista could take you to the Met tomorrow,"

Mom said. "Albie, you know she's from California? Just moved to the city two weeks ago. You've really never been to the Met before?" she asked the girl.

The girl pushed back the plastic tab on her coffee lid and took a sip. "Maybe you can be my tour guide," she told me.

I squinted my eyes at her. There was a tiny chunk of hair, woven into the very back of her braid, that was neon pink. It matched the checks in her shirt. I wondered if Mom had seen it. Probably not, or I bet she never would've picked her for my nanny. Dad would hate it.

"Okay," I told Calista.

lights. camera.

Erlan Kasteev has always been my best friend, since six years ago, which was when we met. Lucky for both of us we live in the same building, on the same floor even. My family is 8A, and his is 8F. Which makes it easy to know if he's home, because I can check for his bedroom light from my kitchen window.

I knocked on Erlan's door, and one of his sisters answered. Alma, I think. I always had trouble telling his sisters apart, because they were triplets and they looked alike. Not identical—that's what Erlan told me, although they looked identical enough to me. Alma, Roza, and Ainyr. They were all two years older than Erlan, with dark straight hair and dark eyes. Erlan was a triplet too, but I could always tell Erlan apart from Karim and Erik. Erlan said he and his brothers tricked their teachers all the time, and the other kids at our old school. He said they even tricked his parents once. But not me. I always knew. That's because Erlan just looked like Erlan.

"Oh," Alma or whoever said when she saw me at the door. "It's you." Then she screamed over her shoulder, "Erlan! Your lame friend is here!"

Erlan came to the door lickety-split and tugged me down the hall toward the room he shared with his brothers. The Kasteevs' apartment was bigger than ours, but that day it was crowded—stuffed full of people I didn't recognize, and giant bright lights on stands everywhere, and big black camera equipment.

"What's going on?" I asked.

"They started filming already," Erlan whispered, shutting his bedroom door. "Quick, over here." He tugged me to a sort of fort he'd made with an old patchy quilt tied to his and Karim's bunk bed.

"I thought you said they weren't supposed to come till next week."

"*Shh!*" Erlan hissed, tugging the quilt door closed around us. He poked his head out, to make sure no one had followed us, I guess, and then leaned back against the wall. "I made a deal with Mom that no one's allowed to record inside the fort. This is my one secret space. They wrote it on a form and everything. Here, and the bathroom when someone's peeing. Those are the only places they can't go."

Erlan looked very upset. I could tell because his eyes were bugged out huge, which is exactly how they were all the other times he was upset, like when he lost the finals of the regional chess championships last year. I wanted to feel bad for him, but actually I thought the whole TV thing was kind of cool.

"Maybe it will be fun," I told him, "having your own show."

This year, a network was filming a reality show about Erlan's family. It was going to be on the television and the Internet and everything. People were going to follow them around with cameras, everywhere they went, and then other people would watch all the episodes. The whole family would probably have their faces all huge on a billboard, right off the FDR Drive, and everywhere they went, people would know everything about them. I thought it sounded amazing. I asked my parents why we couldn't have a reality show about us, and Dad said, "Because your mother and I didn't have the foresight to have two sets of triplets. Now eat your spinach."

Erlan wrinkled his nose at me, and I watched his face while he thought hard. Sometimes people at school—well, my *old* school, Mountford—thought me and Erlan were related because we were both Asian, and because we spent so much time together, I guess. Once some kid at lunch even asked if we were twins, which made Erlan snort milk up his nose, and I laughed so hard I got a stomach-ache, because Erlan's brother Erik was sitting right across from us. But anyway, we're not. Related, I mean. Erlan's family is Kazakh, from Kazakhstan, and I'm half Korean, half Swiss, so we're not even from the same sort of place. But sometimes people have trouble figuring that stuff out.

"I don't think it will be fun," Erlan told me. "I don't want everybody in the world to watch me pooping!"

"I thought you said they couldn't film you in the bath-room."

"You know what I mean," Erlan said, even though I wasn't sure I did. "I just want to be left alone."

"Oh," I told him. I guessed that made sense. But still. I couldn't help thinking that it would be awfully nice to have people think you were interesting enough to put on TV.

We spent the morning hanging out in Erlan's quilt fort, playing board games. Erlan's favorite game is chess. He's really good at it—he has trophies and everything. But he knows I don't like that one, so he doesn't try to make me play it anymore. Instead we play Operation, and Chutes and Ladders, and sometimes Monopoly or cards. Erlan's sister Roza made fun of us one time (I think it was Roza), and asked how come we only ever played little-kid games, but Erlan told her to just shut up, that she was being a snob. Then he decided he was going to teach me poker, which I sort of liked.

"It's going to be weird at school this year without you there," Erlan said. I was deciding which cards from my hand to trade in. We were playing poker for seashells, and Erlan had more shells than me, but not a lot more. "It's gonna stink, I bet."

"Yeah," I said. But it was hard to feel bad for Erlan when I was feeling so bad for me. He'd still have his brothers, and his sisters too, plus all our other friends. And once his show was on TV, everyone in the world practically would know who he was and love him and think he was cool. And I wasn't going to know *anybody* at my new school. "I bet."

"It's not like Albie's going to Turkey," came a voice from outside the fort. Alma, maybe. "He lives right down the hall."

"Ainyr!" Erlan screeched, pulling back the quilt. So I guess it was Ainyr. "What are you doing? Get out of here!"

Ainyr did not get out of there. She kept standing in the doorway, with her hands on her hips. Behind her in the living room, there were two cameramen and a lady with a clipboard shouting.

"Mom says it's time for you to do your pre-interview. I'm supposed to come get you."

"I'm not doing it."

"You have to," Ainyr told him. "Mom and Dad said. And"—her eyes lit up a little bit—"they want to put *makeup* on you."

Erlan hollered so loudly at that, my ears almost fell off. It was so loud that I couldn't really hear the words he was saying, but I'd bet probably it was something about not wanting to wear makeup.

I took my hands off my ears just in time to hear Ainyr say, "*I* don't care if you want to look like a washed-out ghost on national TV. But you have to do the interview. Mom and Dad said." And then she stormed out of the room, and left the door wide open.

"Come on," I told Erlan when she was gone. He looked upset again, and I didn't like when he was upset. He was my best friend, so it was my job to make him happy. "I'll go with you." And I gave him the Vulcan salute, which was just the four fingers on my right hand making a V. It was from an old TV show that Erlan's dad liked. He tried to make us watch a couple times, and me and Erlan didn't really get it, but we liked the pointy-ear stuff and the Vulcan salute.

Erlan Vulcan-saluted me back, and together we left the tent.

Erlan did the interview, because Karim and Erik refused to pretend to be him, even after he said he'd give them ten dollars. But he didn't let the makeup lady put makeup on him. He told that lady if she even tried to brush his hair, he'd put an ancient Kazakh curse on her. Which I did not know Erlan knew how to do before that, but like my mom says, you learn something new every day. Erlan sat on the couch with Erik and Karim, who answered questions about what it was like to be a triplet, and how they liked living in New York City, all sorts of things. Erik and Karim were the only ones who answered. Erlan scowled at the wall the whole time. I only knew that's what he was doing because his mom kept hissing, "Erlan, stop scowling!" and the woman with the clipboard shook her head at the man with the earpiece and said, "It's fine, we'll edit, keep rolling," and four different people asked, "Erlan, did you have anything you wanted to add?"

He did not.

With all the bright lights on them, Erik and Karim did look a lot less like washed-out ghosts than Erlan did.

I was a good best friend the whole time they were recording the interview. It took a long time, and not just because of the scowling and the hissing. It also took a long time because the lady with the clipboard decided she wanted to move the couch twice, and every time, Erlan and his brothers had to get up, and then all the people with the headsets had to move all the camera equipment and the lights and everything, and then after that, they'd ask the same exact interview questions all over again, and there would be more hissing and more scowling. But the whole time, I stood by the camera and made funny faces at Erlan to cheer him up, which I think was working until the woman with the clipboard pointed at me and said, "Who is this kid? Can we get him out of here? He's in my light." And I had to go home.

That night, when I checked through my kitchen window to see if Erlan's bedroom light was on, just before I went to bed, he spied me checking, and he smiled a tiny smile and gave me the Vulcan salute. I Vulcanned back.

   It was good to know that even if Erlan was about to be a big-time TV star, he was still my best friend.

a perfect summer day.

Calista really was from California. And she didn't know anything about New York.

"How do you know which way is uptown?" she asked me when we were on our way to the Met. Mom said it was such a lovely day, we should walk the twenty blocks. I was thinking if it was such a lovely day, we probably shouldn't spend it in a boring old museum, but I didn't say that. "Why doesn't the subway always stop at every stop? Where do you buy a bus pass? Which way is Brooklyn?" She really didn't know anything.

And so, on our way to the Metropolitan Museum of Art, I taught Calista everything there was to know about New York—the streets and the avenues, express subways, bus stops. It was easy stuff, but maybe not for her, I guess, being from somewhere else. I even told her about all the different boroughs. Manhattan, Brooklyn, Queens, the Bronx, and Staten Island. I could name them all without even counting.

Calista nodded after I named each one, like she was plugging them into her brain for keeps. Then she squinted one eye. "What's a borough?" she asked.

I just shrugged. "Like, a part of the city?" I said. I wondered why I never wondered that before.

"It sounds like a place where moles live," Calista told me. And after that I couldn't stop picturing moles all over New York City, digging tunnels between Manhattan and Queens. I smiled to myself.

"So what's *in* the Met, anyway?" Calista asked while she made us wait for the light to change before we crossed at 70th Street. I told her we didn't have to do that, but she said even if she lived in New York now she wasn't a daredevil, whatever that meant. She made us wait at every single block for the light.

Getting anywhere in California must take *forever*.

Calista was good at asking questions, though, so I didn't mind too much how slow we were going.

"It's mostly boring stuff," I told Calista, about the Met.

We were walking up Park Avenue, halfway to the museum. Park Avenue was my favorite in the spring because of the million zillion tulips in the huge flower beds in the middle of the street—yellow, pink, orange. A giant garden with traffic zooming all around it. In the summer it wasn't anything special, just a regular avenue. "The Temple of Dandruff is pretty cool, though."

"Temple of Dandruff?"

I frowned. "Maybe it's called something else. I don't remember. Anyway, that one's pretty cool, and the armor stuff"—Calista made us wait at another light, while everyone in the entire universe crossed in front of us and did not get hit by any cars—"but all the rest of it is more boring than anything." I didn't even *mention* the forty-two thousand old oil paintings of stuffy dead guys with fur collars no one cared about. Looking at all of those could make a person keel over, just from how boring they were. Plus, there were, like, six whole rooms filled with chairs.

Chairs.

The Natural History Museum was way better. The Sea, Air, and Space Museum was even better than that. It was my favorite of all. I'd only been there once, with my dad a year and a half ago, but I still had my model airplane I got in the gift shop. A real A-10 Thunderbolt. Me and Dad were even almost done putting it together.

The walk signal came on, and after checking both ways twice, Calista let us cross. At least she didn't make me hold her hand like I was some kind of baby that had never crossed a street before.

"So why are we going to this museum," Calista asked, "if you think it's so boring?"

I shrugged. "Mom said you'd never been there."

"I've never been *anywhere*," Calista said. "At least not in New York. So why would I want to go somewhere boring?"

I thought about that. She had a pretty good point, actually.

"What do you like to do?" she asked me.

"Me?"

She laughed. "Yes, you. What do you like to do in New York City? You can be my tour guide. We can do anything you want."

"Anything?"

And that's how we spent the perfect summer day in New York City, doing all the best things I like to do. We went to the pet store on 81st and Madison and looked at the puppies. We even got to go to the back to play with them, because Calista said we were thinking of buying one, which was a lie, but Calista said it was okay. We went to Duane Reade and had a contest to see who could find the ugliest sunglasses (I won), then we bought two squirt guns and had a water fight in the park (she won). We got soft-serve cones at Tasti D-Lite and then new ones from the Mr. Softee truck, to see which ones we liked better. (I liked Mr. Softee, which I already knew, but Calista picked Tasti D-Lite because she said they had better sprinkles.) We bought soft pretzels from the cart in the park, even though I told Calista they tasted like the soggy cardboard from the bottom of the pizza box. We fed leftover pretzels to the ducks. We got chased by a goose.

And then, at the end of the perfect day, I taught Calista how to hail a cab.

"You gotta look at the number on the top," I told her, "to see if it's lit up. Otherwise there's a person in it already. And if it says 'off duty' you can't get that one either."

Calista nodded. "And I just stick my hand out, like this?"

"Yeah, but maybe go further out, because no one's going to see you there."

"You want me to stand in the *street*?" Calista shrieked.

"That's how my dad always does it."

Calista hailed six cabs, all by herself. When they stopped to pick us up, Calista told them, "Thank you very much, but I changed my mind." They growled and pulled back onto the street. One man said a not very nice word.

We took the bus home, and I showed Calista the cord to pull when she wanted the driver to stop. It had only been a couple hours, but I was already hoping that Calista would last longer than any of my other nannies (even if she wasn't really a nanny, or a babysitter either), because I'd already figured out that she was way more fun than any of them. Nannies didn't last long, though, I knew that. They either moved or had their own kids or got other jobs that paid more money. Mom said that was just how it worked with nannies.

"Thanks for showing me around, Albie," Calista told me as we walked past Thom at the front desk of our building and into the elevator. "You're a very good tour guide."

"I am?"

"Yeah." Calista punched the button for the eighth floor, and the elevator doors closed. "You're real smart, you know that?"

Smart.

That's what she said.

"How was the Met?" Mom asked when we came inside. She was sitting at her laptop at the table. I didn't see Dad anywhere.

I opened up my mouth to tell her about the park and the ice cream and the goose, but Calista answered before me.

"It was great," she told my mom. "Not boring at all."

And my mom didn't see, but Calista winked at me.

"Well, that's nice," my mom said, and she turned back to her computer. "You enjoyed yourself, Albie?"

I looked from my mom, staring at her computer screen, back to Calista.

"Yeah," I said, and I put a big grin across my face, to match Calista's. "I had a great time."

noticing.

I'm good at noticing things. I've always been good at noticing. Mrs. Lancaster back at Mountford told me. She said that was one of my "strengths," that I always picked up on tiny details that no one else ever saw. She said, "Albie, if you had any skill at language, you might've made a very fine writer." That's what she said.

Here are some things I notice.

I notice that even though my best friend, Erlan, is the same exact age as me (which is ten), I'm two whole inches taller. My arms reach way farther when I stretch too.

That's a thing anybody could notice, though. That one's easy.

I notice that I can fill a water balloon at the drinking fountain in the park almost twice as fast as Erlan. He always gets the knot twisted around his finger and spills water all down his shirt and has to start over, and I can always tie mine no problem.

That's an easy one to notice too.

But I bet that no one else but me ever notices that when Erlan's mom says to count out ten peanut butter crackers for a snack, Erlan always gets his on his plate just a little bit faster than me.

Just a little bit.

And I bet that no one ever noticed either that when me and Holly Martin would do library helpers every other Monday, she always finished her stack of books to put back on the shelf a couple minutes before me. Just a couple minutes. It was the same amount of books, but it was always a couple minutes. Every time. I think I figured out why Holly was faster. Because I watched her when she was putting the books away, and her mouth didn't move at all the way mine does when I'm saying the alphabet in my head. I think maybe Holly didn't have to say the alphabet in her head. I think maybe she just knew the order somehow, without even saying it.

I bet no one noticed either that when Mr. Onorato came in for science last year and asked who thought the tall, skinny glass could hold more water than the short fat one, I was the only kid who raised my hand wrong. I bet no one noticed, because I raised it really quick, and then I noticed nobody else had their hand up, so I put mine down. And I sit in the back anyway.

(It was a trick question besides, because both glasses held the same exact amount of water. Somehow everyone else knew that already.)

I bet no one even noticed I stopped raising my hand in class.

I don't think anyone but me notices any of those things. I'm really good at noticing.

I hope I'll always be a better noticer than everybody else.

lunch.

Erlan's sister Ainyr told me that the hardest part of going to a new school would be lunch. "If you don't have anybody to sit with," she told me, "then everyone will think you're a loser. If you sit with other loser kids, then everyone will think you're a loser too. If you sit with kids who are way cooler than you, and they don't want to sit with you, then they'll think you're a loser. You have to find kids to sit with who are just a *little* bit cooler than you, but not too much. Then everyone will think you're cool too, but not trying too hard."

When she said all that, it made me really scared. Because it sounded super hard to figure all that out, and what if I messed up?

Lucky for me, at my new school, everybody had to eat lunch with their same class, so I didn't worry too much once I figured that out. Everybody in Mrs. Rouse's class sat at one long table in the middle of the cafeteria. Mostly it was boys on one side, and girls on the other, but it was mixed up a little bit.

I was sitting next to a girl who was tons shorter than me, even sitting down. Her feet didn't quite reach the floor. I looked at her lunch as she pulled it out of her brown paper lunch bag. Turkey sandwich with no crusts, cut at an angle. A box of apple cranberry juice. Carrot sticks. It looked like a healthy lunch, but loads better than mine. I had leftover kimchi and a cold bagel with cream cheese, which is what Mom gives me when she forgets to make my lunch the day before. I have that lunch a lot. I looked around the table. Nobody else had kimchi. Almost everybody had sandwiches. I zipped the kimchi back inside my puffy green lunch sack.

While I chewed my bagel, I looked around the table and tried to figure out who Erlan's sister Ainyr would think was cool, and who she would say was a loser. But I couldn't really tell. Everybody sort of just looked like a fifth-grader. There was a boy with spiky hair and a kid with a skateboarding shirt. One of the girls had a panda lunch box, which at my old school would be lame, but she seemed like she had a lot of friends, so maybe here panda lunch boxes were okay. I wondered who made up the rules about what was lame and what wasn't, and who was cool and who was a loser. If somebody told me what the rules were, I'd be fine.

While I was thinking all that, the girl next to me, the short one with the healthy-but-good lunch, pulled another thing out of her lunch bag.

"Gummy bears?" I said. "Cool." I love gummy bears.

The girl looked up at me and smiled. It was kind of a funny smile, actually, like she was surprised I was talking to her. But before she could say anything, the boy across from me who was wearing the skateboard shirt—I think Mrs. Rouse called him Darren—said, "Ew, Albie, don't talk to Buh-Buh-Buh-Betsy."

I don't know why he said her name like that—Buh-Buh-Buh-Betsy. But when I looked at the girl, it seemed like she definitely didn't like it. Her shoulders were sunk down, and her face was red, and somehow she looked even smaller than before.

"Don't call her that," I said to the skateboard shirt boy. Darren. "That's mean." I didn't know *why* it was mean, but sometimes you could tell that a person wasn't being nice, even if you weren't sure how.

"Ew, Albie!" Darren said. "Is Buh-Buh-Buh-Betsy your *girlfriend*?" And then he laughed like that was so funny, and so did all the boys next to him, and practically the whole other side of the lunch table. Then Darren tossed a potato chip toward me, and it stuck to my shirt. And even though it didn't hurt, because it was just a potato chip, I knew that that *definitely* wasn't nice.

The whole other side of the lunch table laughed again.

I think maybe a couple other kids might have almost started to toss potato chips at me too, because I could tell they thought it looked like fun, but just then, one of the lunch duty aides came over and got mad at Darren for throwing food. Darren glared at me the whole time, like it was my fault he threw a potato chip at me and got in trouble, and the whole other side of the lunch table glared too.

That's when I figured out that at P.S. 183, Darren was the one who wrote the rules.

So it turned out that Erlan's sister Ainyr was right. Lunch was the hardest part of the day. But it wasn't all bad.

After Darren and his friends finished glaring at me and went to the playground, I looked back at the table, and there, on a napkin next to my puffy green lunch sack, was a gummy bear. A red one. And everyone knows that red gummy bears are the best ones.

I looked over at the girl next to me. "Thanks," I told her. And I popped the gummy bear in my mouth.

She smiled. Somehow she didn't look so small when she smiled.

stutter.

I figured out why Darren and those other mean kids called the girl with the gummy bears Buh-Buh-Buh-Betsy. It was because she has trouble saying words sometimes, especially beginnings, like *b*'s and *t*'s and *k*'s. I noticed it in class when Mrs. Rouse asked her to read a passage out loud from the textbook. The boys started snickering, and her face turned bright red, and her voice got really quiet, so quiet you could hardly hear her, until finally Mrs. Rouse said, "Thank you, Betsy. That was wonderful."

Betsy doesn't talk too much.

I asked Calista about it, and Calista said it sounded like Betsy had a stutter, which can make talking hard.

I decided I liked Betsy. She gave me gummy bears at lunch without me even asking. We even picked each other for library partners. And when I got confused when Mrs. Rouse was explaining about the online card catalog, Betsy didn't make fun of me. She just pointed to the right place where I was supposed to click. I didn't mind that Betsy didn't talk too much. Because it can be hard sometimes, saying what you mean. And I thought maybe I understood her most of the time anyway.

einstein.

On Saturday afternoon, Mom and I went for hot choco-late at the pastry place on Lexington. I always got hot chocolate, and she got coffee, and we picked one dessert from the case and split it. Sometimes it was crowded there, but it was my favorite place to go because there were giant hunks of stale bread with slits cut in them for the menus to slide into, and I thought that was funny. Also, the food was good.

After we were finished with our éclair (which is just a fancy donut, really) but still sipping our drinks, a woman came up who I guess Mom knew from work.

"And this must be Albie!" she said when she was done

hugging Mom. The lady was wearing too much eye makeup. But I was polite, so I said hi.

"Hi."

Then she hugged me too, which I didn't like.

"It's so nice to meet you, Albie."

I smiled a smile without teeth.

"I bet you're a whiz in school," the lady told me. I guess I looked confused when she said that, because then she said, "Well, when you share a name with one of the smartest men who ever lived, how could you not be?"

I tilted my head to the side and probably looked more confused.

"Albert Einstein," she explained. And when she said it, she looked like I really should've known that. Like maybe I wasn't so smart after all.

I waited for Mom to say something about that, but when I looked up at her, she was smiling a smile without teeth. "It was lovely running into you, Theresa," she said, and then she hugged the lady again, and I had to hug her too, but after that the lady went away, which was good.

"My name's not Albert," I said when I was sitting down again, back to sipping my hot chocolate. "It's Albin."

"I know that, Albie," Mom said. "I named you, remember?" She finished the rest of her coffee. "You about ready?"

"Yeah, almost."

I let the last sip of hot chocolate sit on my tongue for a little bit before I swallowed it down, and then Mom and I headed home.

almost, albie.

My whole life, I've always been an almost.

"Almost, Albie."

"Almost."

I was an almost in kindergarten when I asked if I could use markers at art time, instead of just crayons.

"Almost, Albie," the art teacher said. "Let's wait until your grip is a little stronger."

I was an almost in first grade when I wanted to walk our dog, Biscuit.

"Almost, Albie," my mom said. "He still tugs too hard for you."

I was an almost in second grade after I spent a whole weekend practicing my sounding-out words so I could move up to the red reading group.

"Almost, Albie," Miss Langhoff told me. "You have a tiny ways to go."

I was an almost in third grade too, when my poem wasn't picked for the wall for Parents' Night.

"Almost, Albie," Mr. Vidal said. "I almost put yours up. But there were so many to choose from."

By fourth grade, I was an almost every day.

"Almost, Albie."

That's what they tell me.

"Almost."

"Almost."

Always, *always* almost.

a real a-10 thunderbolt.

Me and my dad went to the Sea, Air, and Space Museum together once, when I was nine. We spent the whole day together, me and him. It was the best day. Dad even had fun too, I think. He said he did. Afterward he said he wasn't so sorry the subway broke down and got us stuck there, all the way over on the west side of Manhattan, where no cabdriver would ever dream of picking us up.

Dad bought me a model airplane from the gift shop, a real A-10 Thunderbolt. He said he'd help me put it together. He hasn't had a lot of time lately, but one of these days, he will. It will be a lot of fun.

math club.

M rs. Rouse signed me up for math club. She did it
without even asking me, which I thought wasn't very
fair. I told her I didn't want to be in any math club, because
math is the worst subject out of any subject in the school.
Only I didn't exactly say the part about math being awful,
because she taught math, so that might make her sad. Even
if she did deserve it, because of signing me up for math club
without even asking me.

"I think you'll like it, Albie, really," Mrs. Rouse told me,
which was what grown-ups said right before they made you

do something that stunk. I wrinkled my nose. "Just give it a shot, all right?"

I guess I didn't have much choice, now, did I?

The one good thing about math club was that it took place during my regular math time, so I only had to do math once a day instead of twice, like I was worried about. The club leader's name was Mr. Clifton, and there were five other kids in fourth-period math club, from all different grades.

The first thing I noticed about Mr. Clifton was that he smiled a lot. There were basketball posters all over the walls, that was the next thing I noticed. Which I thought was good, because I was worried that a teacher who was in charge of math club might only like math and nothing else, and that would be terrible. I didn't know a whole lot about basketball, but it seemed way better than math anyway, so I figured Mr. Clifton was probably all right.

What happened in math club the first day was that Mr. Clifton gave us all one goldfish cracker and then asked us how many we had altogether. Which was easy. Even I knew that one. It was six. That wasn't math, it was counting. Then Mr. Clifton gave us all another goldfish cracker, and asked us again. He kept giving us more and more goldfish crackers, and then we all put our piles together in the middle of the table and helped each other count them. Savannah was the fastest counter, and this boy Jacob was the slowest. I was second-slowest, but no one seemed to care.

All the kids were nice.

When math club was over, Mr. Clifton let us eat the crackers.

"You guys eat like sharks!" Mr. Clifton said as we gobbled up the last of the crackers. "You sure you all got enough breakfast?"

I got back to Mrs. Rouse's room just in time for recess, and she said that as long as I went to math club every single day, I didn't have to do math homework with the rest of the class. That's when I told Mrs. Rouse that math club maybe wasn't so bad after all and I wasn't mad at her for signing me up for it.

"Thanks, Albie," she said. "I appreciate you telling me that."

"They should change the name, though," I said.

"Oh?" Mrs. Rouse asked.

"Yeah. Instead of 'math club' they should call it 'cracker club,' because we didn't do any math at all."

Mrs. Rouse just smiled.

an empty tin can.

Calista could make friends with an empty tin can—that's what she told me her boyfriend said about her. I don't know why her boyfriend thought Calista would want to be friends with an empty tin can, but anyway, he was probably right. I figured that out after we stopped at the bodega downstairs on our way home from school one day and she started talking to Hugo, the old man who owns the store.

Also, I didn't know Calista had a boyfriend. Why hadn't she ever told me before that she had a boyfriend?

"You wouldn't happen to have any bottle caps, would you?" Calista asked Hugo while I studied the donut case on the counter to decide which one I wanted most. Mom said my limit was one donut per week, but I think she forgot to tell Calista that, because Calista let me have one almost every day, as long as I spent my own allowance on it.

"Bottle caps?" Hugo asked. He had a thick accent, but I couldn't tell from where. He had lots of curly gray hair and a big wide nose, and he was very friendly. I was glad he was our bodega owner and not the guy who worked at the one on 62nd Street. Erlan and I went in there once to see if they had Smarties, and that guy yelled at us, "No parents? Get out!" Even though Erlan's mom was right outside on her cell phone.

"Yeah," Calista told Hugo. "I'm collecting bottle caps for an art project."

I pressed my nose close to the plastic case and studied the jelly donut and the twist with chocolate frosting. I was feeling more like a jelly donut, but the twist looked fresher. While I was thinking, Calista tried to explain to Hugo about her art project. By the time I settled on a plain glazed, Calista was behind the counter, showing him pictures of her "work in progress" on her phone.

"That's pretty good!" he told her, and she smiled big.

I lifted the lid of the plastic case and grabbed a paper tissue to pick out my donut. I wondered why Calista had never told *me* she needed bottle caps before. I found bottle caps all over the place.

Hugo rang up my donut on the register, and I pulled my dollar out of my pocket.

"You come in here a lot, don't you?" he asked me. And when I nodded, he stretched his hand across the counter. "I'm Hugo."

"I know," I told him. "It says so on your name tag."

"Albie!" Calista nudged me in the side. "He gets shy," she told Hugo. Which was not true. She stretched her hand out to shake Hugo's, which is when I realized that's what I probably should have done. "I'm Calista," she told him, and they shook.

"Nice to meet you, Calista," Hugo told her. "You too, Albie." But he didn't try to shake my hand again, which made me mad, because that time I was all ready. I put my dollar on the counter and shrugged at him. "Well, see you two tomorrow!" he said.

Calista said good-bye, but I didn't.

"He's nice," she told me as we squeezed into the elevator.

I pushed the button for floor eight, and the door closed. I stared at the glazed donut in the paper tissue in my hand. I wanted to take a giant bite right there, but donuts always tasted better if you waited till you were home first.

"How come you never told me you had a boyfriend?" I asked Calista.

Calista was putting her phone back in her pocket. "Didn't I?" she asked.

"No," I said. And I wasn't sure why, but that made me madder than not shaking Hugo's hand.

I took a bite of the donut.

jokes.

Every day at the beginning of math club, Mr. Clifton told us a new joke. He'd wait until we were all in our seats, and then he'd raise his white eyebrows, and smile just a little bit, and say the first part of the joke.

"Why are math books always so sad?"

That was the one from Thursday. I didn't know the answer, but no one else did either, so I didn't feel bad. Pretty much no one ever knew the answer.

You could always tell when Mr. Clifton was about to say the punch line, because he'd clear his throat and look like he was about to say something super serious.

"Because," he said, his head tilted low so that he was looking at us all from over the tops of his glasses, "they have so many *problems*."

That one made us all laugh—well, all except Savannah. She hardly laughed at any of the jokes, only the *really* really funny ones. I laughed at almost all of them.

When Mr. Clifton saw that we liked that joke pretty well, he nodded, very serious, and went behind his desk to write something in his notebook. "Use again next year," he mumbled to himself as he wrote.

The only thing I didn't like about Mr. Clifton's jokes was that they were always about math.

ten words.

I studied for the spelling test every Thursday. Calista helped me. Every single Thursday. We went over all the words. Calista even made flash cards sometimes, with pictures on them, so I would remember the words and the way to spell them. *Growth.* G-R-O-W-T-H. That flash card had a flower on it, for *grow* spelled the normal way, like a flower grows, and then after that, there was a boy smiling with all his teeth, for the *th* sound that comes at the end of *teeth*.

So how come I could remember that when I was doing flash cards with Calista, but when it came to the test on

Friday, I wrote *groth,* because I forgot how to spell *grow* like a flower because I got nervous? Anyway, sometimes *o* makes the *ow* sound even when the *w*'s not there, like in *note.* There's no *w* in *note.*

There are ten words on the test every Friday. Ten words. No matter how hard I study on Thursday, I never get more than four of them right.

some bug.

Darren Ackleman brought in a bug for Science Friday. It was a dead bug, a beetle, he said, even though it sort of looked like a cockroach. It was the biggest bug I'd ever seen, bigger than two giant pink erasers stuck together. It was trapped in a small clear box, and it was black with yellow splotches. Its head was crazy. It looked like it had horns, real horns, sticking right out the top. Lila screamed when Darren held it up, and Josie made fake barfing sounds, and Hillary and two other girls pretended like they were fainting, but all the boys thought it was really cool. Some of them even got out of their desks and rushed to the front of the room to see the bug closer. It got so loud in the classroom that Mrs. Rouse had to say, "Now, now, boys and girls!" in her very stern loud voice, and flash the lights on and off. But even then, it was hard to settle down.

After a minute, the teacher from the classroom next door, Mr. Harrison, poked his head inside and said, "Everything okay in here? It sounds like a stampede of yaks."

And Mrs. Rouse shook her head and said, real tired, "Nope, only a dead bug."

At that point Mr. Harrison said, "That must be some bug," and after he saw it, he asked Mrs. Rouse if he could bring his sixth-graders in from next door to look at it, because he thought they'd really love it too. So then all the sixth-graders came into the room and filed past Darren Ackleman at the front and screamed and hooted and shouted about the bug, until Mrs. Rouse made them sit down in the aisles between our desks so Darren could finish his Science Friday. Darren stood up at the front, grinning like it was his birthday or something while he explained all about the bug, how his dad bought it from a shop that sells bugs and skulls and all sorts of weird stuff that made the girls all shriek again, and how it was real expensive, and how his dad said he trusted Darren to take it to school for Science Friday, because he knew Darren was always really careful.

I did not want to like the bug. I did not want to like the

bug because I didn't like Darren. But it was so *cool,* with its horns and everything, and I really wanted to count the yellow spots on its back, so when Mrs. Rouse said if we could all stay calm and remain in our seats, then Darren could come through the aisles and let us look at the bug more closely, I decided I would take a turn looking. I decided I could like the bug and not like Darren.

Betsy liked the bug too, I could tell. She leaned forward in her seat beside me, trying to see better, and when Darren squeezed through her aisle, she peered down to look at it.

"Out of the way, Buh-Buh-Buh-Betsy," Darren hissed as he stepped over a sixth-grader's legs. I heard him. "I'm trying to get through." And she didn't get to see the bug at all.

I got to see the bug a pretty long time, because the sixth-grader who was sitting in the aisle next to me grabbed the case right out of Darren's hands and stared at it for a while, and probably because the kid was so big, Darren didn't tell him to give it back. So I got to see, right over the big kid's shoulder.

It was a cool bug.

"Seven," I told Betsy when we were on our way to lunch. We were walking through the hallways at the back of the lunch line, like usual.

"Suh-seven w-what?" Betsy asked.

"That's how many yellow dots there were on the bug's back," I told her. "I counted. I thought you might be wondering."

Betsy didn't say anything about that—Betsy didn't usually say much of anything, so I was used to it. But she smiled at me, so I could tell she was happy about the spots. And at lunch she gave me three red gummy bears.

"Did you know there's a kind of cockroach that hisses?" I told Betsy while we ate. Some girls would be grossed out talking about bugs during lunch, but not Betsy. I could tell she thought it was cool, because her eyebrows went up on her face as soon as I said that about the hissing. "I saw it on TV," I told her. "Whenever you touch one spot on their back, they hiss real loud, just like this." And I made a hissing noise, just like the cockroach I saw on TV, right through my teeth. And Betsy giggled, so I hissed louder. Then she poked me in the back, like I was a cockroach, and I hissed. Every time she poked me, I hissed, and soon we were both laughing so hard we were almost crying, and I could barely get the hisses out. Betsy snorted and slapped her hand over her mouth, embarrassed, but that just made us laugh harder.

"What are you two retards *doing* over there?" Darren said all of a sudden. And just like that, me and Betsy stopped laughing. That's when we realized that everybody was staring at us.

Everybody.

"What are you looking at, dummy?" Darren asked me. He said it real mean, like I was the one who'd done something to him, even though he was the one who called me and Betsy bad names.

I looked down at my lunch. Next to me, I could tell Betsy was breathing really hard, like she did when she was trying not to cry.

After Darren and his friends left the lunch table to go outside and our side of the table was mostly empty, Betsy nudged me with her elbow.

"Yeah?" I said.

Then Betsy talked real soft, so only I could hear her.

"If D-D-Darren was a b-b-b-bug," she said slowly, "I'd st-step on him."

A smile stretched across my face. I liked that idea. A lot. "Yeah," I told her. "Me too."

And after that day at lunch, every time Darren said something mean, or looked at us funny, or cut in front of one of us in line, me and Betsy would turn to each other and, real quiet so no one else could hear, we'd make a little *hissssssss*. And I wasn't sure about Betsy, but that always made me feel just a little bit better, like I was squashing Darren Ackleman in my head, even if I couldn't squash him in real life.

erlan's
birthday.

Mom said I should have bought Erlan a chess set for his birthday, but I told her he likes lots of things besides just chess. I thought we should get him Rock 'Em Sock 'Em Robots. She also said, "Don't you think we should get something for Karim and Erik? It's their birthday too, you know." I had sort of forgot about it being Karim and Erik's birthday, but then I figured that made sense, because of how they were triplets. But I didn't think I needed to get them presents. They weren't really my friends—just Erlan was. He was the only one of them who came to *my* birthday party. Mom tried to argue for a while, but then she saw how much Rock 'Em Sock 'Em Robots cost, and she said she supposed one present would be fine.

On Saturday I wrapped Erlan's present myself and then walked across the hall right at twelve o'clock, right when it said on the invitation that his party was going to start. I didn't have to buzz the buzzer because the door was already open. There was a man I'd never seen before with a headset and a clipboard standing in the doorway, and he stared at me the whole time I walked toward him. He looked like he was bored.

I thought the man would say something when I got to the door, but he didn't, so I figured I had to start. "Um, hi," I said.

"Name?" he said, like he was asking a question.

"Erlan," I told him.

He looked down at his list. "Last name?" He said that like it was a question too.

"Kasteev," I said. I thought he should probably know that already, since he was standing in the Kasteevs' doorway and working on their TV show, but he asked, so I told him.

The man sighed like he was really annoyed and looked up from his list. "What's *your* name, smart guy?" he said. But the way he rolled his eyes, it made it seem like maybe he didn't really think I was a smart guy at all. I thought I was the one who should be annoyed at him, though, because if he wanted to know *my* name, that's what he should have said in the first place.

"Albie Schaffhauser," I said, standing on my tiptoes to look at the list upside down. "Albin."

The man made a check on his list with his pen and then pulled a piece of paper out from under the list on his clipboard. "You need a parent or guardian to sign a release form," he said, handing me the paper.

I stared at it for a while, confused, then I looked up at the door again. Inside Erlan's apartment, there were tons of people walking around, setting food on tables, moving furniture, turning on great big light stands. I saw a couple kids I knew from Mountford, but most were grown-ups I'd never met before.

I didn't see Erlan anywhere.

"I'm just here for Erlan's birthday party," I told the man. I never needed to sign a piece of paper to get in Erlan's apartment before.

"Sorry, kid," the man told me. He didn't really sound very sorry, though. "I can't let anyone in without a release form. If your face ends up on camera and a parent hasn't signed off, the company could get sued."

I was still confused. "I'm here for Erlan's birthday," I said again. Last year we played laser tag in the park. That was better than this already.

"Sorry." He still wasn't sorry. "Call your folks and get them to come sign the form. Or a guardian. Then you can go inside."

I didn't have to call my parents because they were just

down the hall. Well, my mom wasn't home. It was only my dad, and he didn't like when I bothered him when he was on his treadmill, but I didn't really have a choice.

"What?" he kept shouting while he ran, every time I tried to show him the paper and explain. "What?" Finally he snapped off the TV and shut down the treadmill and glared at me. "Albie, you know I only get five minutes to myself a day," he said, super angry, even though I didn't do anything—it was the man with the clipboard. Dad took a long glug of water.

"I know," I said. "But"—I held out the form again—"the man at the door wouldn't let me in."

Dad snatched the form out of my hand, still angry. But then while he was reading the paper, I started to think maybe he was mad at the form.

"Come with me," he said, and he jumped off the treadmill and stormed out the door. I grabbed the Rock 'Em Sock 'Em Robots even tighter and followed him.

I stood outside Erlan's door for ten whole minutes while Dad argued with the man in the headset. I could see the sweat on the back of my dad's T-shirt from running before. He waved the paper in the man's face while he shouted at him.

"Well, I *don't* give my consent for my son to be on camera!" Dad hollered. I could tell he was extra angry, because the angrier he got, the more spit flew out of his mouth when he yelled, and there was a *lot* of spit coming out at the man with the headset. "I'm his *father,* and that means protecting my kid. And my kid will *not* participate in this reality circus!" A bunch of people from inside came to the door to see what was happening, and a few kids I knew from Mountford who got off the elevator had to wait behind us in the hallway until my dad was done being mad. "You can't stop my son from going to this birthday party," he said. "He and Erlan have been friends for eight years, and I'm not going to let some idiotic television show get in the way of that." Erlan and I had only been friends for six years, and Dad kept saying *ER-lan* instead of *Er-LAN,* which is the way you're supposed to say it. But I didn't think that part mattered so much.

Finally the man with the headset said he had to talk to his producer, and he was gone for a long time. But when he came back, he told me I could come inside.

"And you're giving me your word you will not film my son?" my dad asked.

"You couldn't pay me to," the man said, rolling his eyes as he checked the forms of the kids who'd come up behind us in the hallway.

"I have a good lawyer, you know," my dad said.

"I'm sure you do," the man told him.

Dad hugged my shoulder and told me to have a good time. Even though he was still sweaty, I let him hug me anyway.

"Thanks," I said, because I was glad he was protecting

me, like he said, even if I didn't really get how he was doing that. Also I wondered why all the other kids' dads didn't seem to care so much about protecting *their* kids. But I figured that was just one of those things I didn't understand.

I went inside.

I didn't even know Erlan and his brothers had so many friends. Practically everyone I'd ever met at Mountford was there, plus their parents. There was hardly enough room for everyone, with the TV cameras and the lights and everything, so all the parents were crammed against the walls while the kids played games sitting on the living room floor. We played musical chairs, but instead of chairs, you had to sit on paper plates, because there weren't enough chairs, and it was super hard to run because you had to dodge the two camera guys, who didn't even seem to care that they were getting in the way. I did pretty good at musical plates, though. I got out third from last. Every time the camera came near me, the red-haired lady who seemed like she was in charge would shout out "No release!" and then whoever had the camera would zoom toward a different kid. Which was fine with me because it made running a whole lot easier.

Ainyr won the game.

It seemed like everybody was dressed nicer than usual, even Erlan. Normally he wore shorts and T-shirts, but today he had on a shirt with buttons all down it, and a tie even.

"Mom made me," he said when I asked about it. "I said I just wanted to look like myself."

The camera people made Erlan and his brothers blow out the candles on their birthday cake three times, because they said they couldn't get the angle right. Just before they were about to blow them out the second time, the red-haired lady pointed to me, right by Erlan's shoulder, and shouted, "No release!" And then they made me move across the room. Gretchen from Mountford said she felt sorry for me about that, but I didn't care so long as I got cake and ice cream. That part was taking forever.

I wondered if you blew your birthday candles out three times, did that mean you got three wishes?

When it was time for presents, Erlan got ten new chess sets.

After the party was over and most of the kids had gone home, Erlan and I hung out in the quilt fort in his bedroom and played Rock 'Em Sock 'Em Robots. Erlan kept shouting "No release!" right before he attacked me with the red bot, and then I'd holler "No release!" even louder and attack him right back with my blue one. I knocked his block clean off eight times.

It was the best part of the party.

reading
log.

Mom thumbed through my homework folder while our dinner whirled in the microwave. I looked at the time. Four minutes thirty-seven seconds to go. My stomach growled.

"Albie," Mom said slowly, pulling a sheet out of the folder, "is this your reading log?"

I adjusted the napkins on the table so they were perfectly straight against the corners, just the way Dad liked, even though he was working late again, so he wouldn't be there to see it. "Yep," I said. I tried to wait until Mom started congratulating me on all my good reading to start smiling, but I couldn't help it. A hint of a grin snuck onto my face. We only had to read for fifteen minutes a night, but the past four days I'd read for twenty at least. On Thursday I even read for *forty*, which I never even thought was possible, unless you were Grandpa Park with his newspaper.

But for some reason, Mom didn't seem happy like she should have been. "What is this?" she asked. And for a second, I thought she'd found some sort of mashed-up banana in my backpack or something, that was how disgusted her question sounded. But there wasn't any mashed-up banana. She was still looking at my reading log. She held it out to me.

My eyes scanned down past where Mrs. Rouse had written "Great reading, Albie!" But I didn't see anything that looked mashed-up-banana disgusting.

"What?" I asked.

Mom flicked the paper back to her own eyeballs. "What on earth are these books you've been reading, Albie?" she said. "*The Adventures of Captain Underpants? Captain Underpants and the Attack of the Talking Toilets? The Invasion of the Potty Snatchers?*"

"Yeah," I said. I still didn't get why she was mad, and when Mom got like that—confusing mad—it was best to talk slow. "The Captain Underpants books. They're really funny." The only problem with them was that their titles were so long, it took me forever to write them on my reading log. But it was worth it.

I set the forks down on the table and moved to the backpack. I pulled a book out for her to see. *Captain Underpants and the Perilous Plot of Professor Poopypants.* "I've read four already." Calista had gotten them for me from the library, which I was about to tell my mom, but for some reason at the last minute, I decided not to. "Look at the pictures," I said instead.

Mom skimmed through the book so fast, I was pretty sure she didn't even notice the flipbooks, which are the funniest parts. "Albie," she said slowly. Her forehead was wrinkled up like it was at Dad sometimes when they talked about who was supposed to do the grocery shopping, but I still didn't get why. We weren't talking about grocery shopping. "You're way too old for these books." She flipped the book open again, to a page where Professor Pippy P. Poopypants is getting really mad about everyone making fun of his name. It's funny because he's a scientist, but also he has a really terrible name. Mom held the page up so I could see. "Look at these drawings," she said. "This is for babies."

I didn't think the book was for babies at all, because for one thing, babies can't read.

"You're in fifth grade, Albie," Mom said. "You should be reading books for fifth-graders."

The timer on the microwave went off then, but Mom

didn't pull out our enchilada dinners. Instead she tossed *Captain Underpants* on a pile of mail on the counter and walked off down the hall. I stood at the table, just waiting. I stared at the enchilada dinner sitting inside the dark microwave. I wanted to take it out and start eating, because I wasn't sure where Mom went and my stomach was growling again, but last time I tried to pull a dinner out of the microwave, I got burned by the steam and Mom got mad at me for being careless.

"Here," Mom said when she finally walked back into the kitchen. She was holding a different book, a new one. She handed it to me.

"*Johnny Tr*—" I tried to sound the title out, but it was tricky looking.

"*Johnny Tremain*," Mom said. "I read it when I was in fifth grade, and I loved it. Now *there's* a book for kids your age."

I turned the book over in my hands. It was thick. Long. Too long. I opened it up. The words were tiny, and there weren't any pictures.

It did not look nearly as good as *Captain Underpants*.

"I want you to read at least one chapter tonight for your reading log, okay?" Mom said. I must've been frowning on accident, because then she said, "Just try it, Albie. I bet you'll love it."

I didn't say anything.

"Now, why are we just standing here? Didn't the microwave beep? Let's eat!"

"I was waiting for you to take the food out," I said.

"What, you can't take food out of the microwave by yourself? You're a big kid, Albie. You need to start acting like it."

My stomach was still growling when I took my first bite of the enchilada dinner, but somehow it didn't taste nearly as delicious as I remembered.

I tried to read *Johnny Tremain*. I really did. I read all the words in the first paragraph, and then the second one. Then I started over with the first paragraph.

That book didn't make any sense.

Captain Underpants was still out on the pile of mail in the kitchen, and that book did make sense. Plus it was funny. But *Captain Underpants* was for babies, and I wasn't a baby.

The next morning, when Mrs. Rouse asked for my reading log, I told her I lost it.

east 59th street tv.

No more TV," Calista said. She was feeling grumpy, I could tell, because some days she'd let me watch for way longer than fifteen minutes, pretending she didn't notice that the timer in the kitchen had gone off. Those days, she'd just stay on the couch, legs tucked underneath her, and doodle in her sketchbook while I watched cartoons. But I guess not today.

"Come on, Albie," she said. She snapped shut her sketchbook. "Turn off the TV, okay?"

"Aww," I whined. "But I'm *watching* something."

"Your show ended two minutes ago," Calista told me, getting up to grab the remote. "Right now you're watching a commercial for shower cleaner."

"But it's *interesting*," I argued.

Calista zapped the TV off.

"Can I play Xbox?" I asked her.

"That's a screen," she replied. Which meant no.

I slumped my shoulders down and sunk onto the floor.

"Want to see if Erlan's home?" Calista said. "Maybe he wants to hang out."

"They're taping a big family meeting today, so I can't come over."

Calista thought for a while. "Want to do an art project?"

"No."

"Bake cookies?"

"No."

"Ride bikes?"

"It's eight thirty," I told her. "I'm not allowed on my bike after dark. Plus, only half an hour till stupid bedtime." I shouldn't have told her that. Maybe she would've forgotten.

"We must be able to think up *something* to do." Calista tapped her finger on her lip the way she did when she was about to be silly. "Want to have a contest to see who can stand on their head the longest? I'll let you win."

I did not laugh. "No," I said.

"Want to eat all the old pickles in the fridge and see if we throw up?"

I did not laugh harder. "No."

"Want to build a cockroach obstacle course?"

That time I laughed a tiny bit. "We don't have cock-roaches," I told Calista.

She nodded at that, very thoughtful. "Well, maybe if we build them an obstacle course, we can get them to show up."

I liked Calista. She could be funny when she wanted to be. But I was not in a funny mood. "What I *want* to do," I told her, "is watch TV."

"I've got it!" she shouted suddenly. Then she raced to the kitchen.

I followed her. "I don't want to bake cookies," I reminded her.

"Don't worry, it's not cookies. I wouldn't *dream* of giving you cookies, Albie."

"Good."

She was pulling flattened-up cardboard boxes out from behind the door of the pantry, where Mom keeps them until Dad finally bundles them so I can take them for recy-cling downstairs. "Perfect," Calista said at last. She pulled out the biggest box, from Mom's last grocery order, and walked past me down the hall.

I followed her some more. She turned into my room and started digging through my desk drawers.

"I said no art projects," I told her when she yanked out a pair of scissors and a black permanent marker.

"Good," she said. "Me neither. I hate art."

That time I knew Calista was lying, because she already told me before that she moved to New York to go to graduate school to study art. And that probably meant she liked it.

But I decided not to tell her I knew she was lying, because by then she was already cutting up the cardboard box, and I sort of wanted to find out why.

"Isn't this better than regular TV?" Calista asked me. We were lying on our stomachs sideways across my bed, squished up next to each other with our feet hanging off because "No Shoes on the Bedspread, Albie" is one of Mom's top ten most serious rules. Calista handed me the remote. "Here, you pick the channel."

It wasn't a real remote control. Calista had made it out of cut-up cardboard and markers. But it turned out she was pretty good at art after all, because the way she decorated it, it looked almost real. I aimed it at the cardboard TV frame she'd taped around my window and pretended to push one of the fake remote control buttons.

"Ooh!" Calista squealed like I'd really done something. "I love this channel!" She pointed out the window.

Our apartment isn't super high, only the eighth floor, but from my window, you sure can see a lot. Two high-rises just across the street, with an even taller one behind that. And if you crane your neck to the left, a view of Park Avenue.

Straight below, you could see all the people leaving the bodega downstairs, and the Laundromat next door.

I guess we did get a lot of channels.

I looked where Calista was pointing. Lots of people had their curtains closed, but not everybody. Right across the street was a blond lady in a blue shirt, standing by the window, stirring something in a bowl in her kitchen. She bounced a little bald baby on her shoulder.

"What do you think she's making?" Calista asked.

I squinted my eyes. "Spaghetti?"

"Quiche?" Calista guessed.

"Brownies?"

"Mmm." She leaned forward. "Maybe she'll let us have some."

I laughed and changed the channel. This time we found an old couple, sitting on the couch. We could tell they were watching TV by the way the light flickered off their faces. We guessed what show it might be until they turned off their TV two minutes later, and then we changed the channel again.

We watched a teenager sitting outside on her fire escape, talking on her cell phone, her feet dangling over the edge to the street below.

We watched a father helping his son brush his teeth at the bathroom sink.

We watched a man hang a bicycle on hooks high on his living room wall.

We watched two women arguing across a dinner table. One of them was crying.

We watched three different people typing at laptops, right in their windows, and not one of them ever looked up to catch us spying.

We even watched a lady give a boy a haircut.

When it was time to get ready for bed, Calista told me she'd help me take the cardboard TV to the recycling, but I said I wanted to keep it up a little longer.

It was sort of nice, to be able to change the channel whenever I wanted.

tuesday.

"What kind of insect is good at math?"

That's the joke Mr. Clifton said on Tuesday. No one knew the answer.

"An account-*ant*!" he told us.

That was a good one. We told Mr. Clifton to use it for the math club kids next year for sure.

caring &
thoughtful
& good.

Most nights Calista was the one who was there for bedtime. She always made sure I had my book and Norm the Bear, even though I didn't need a teddy bear. But I could tell she knew I liked having him anyway. Then she would say good night and close the door and go out to the living room to draw in her sketchbook.

That's what Calista always did at bedtime.

But when Mom was there for bedtime, she tucked me in, even though I was way too old for tucking. She almost always forgot about Norm the Bear, but that was okay. I didn't need a teddy bear anyway. But the thing she never forgot, not once, was that she would lean over and kiss my forehead and say, "I love you, Albie."

"You do?" I would ask, every time, even though I knew the answer.

"Yep," she'd say. "I do. You are caring and thoughtful and good."

Caring and thoughtful and good.

I liked when Mom was there for bedtime.

johnny treeface.

A lbie."
   When I looked up, Calista was holding my reading
log from school. The way she'd said my name wasn't happy.
More like the disappointed way of saying "Albie."

I think I liked that way to say my name the least of any of
them.

"What?" I asked, like I didn't know what she was about
to say next, even though I was pretty sure I did.

"Why is your reading log empty this week?" Which, yep,
was pretty much exactly what I'd thought she was going to

say. "You told me you've been reading at bedtime. Did you forget to mark it down?"

I didn't even look at the paper. I already knew what was on there. Pretty much nothing, that's what was on there. Same as last week's—all blank, except at the top, where Mrs. Rouse had written, "What happened to all your great reading?"

"Albie . . . ," Calista said slowly. Which I guess was supposed to make me want to start talking, but it didn't. "What's going on? Did you run out of Captain Underpants already? Should we go to the library again?"

I shook my head. "Captain Underpants is for babies," I said at last.

Calista raised an eyebrow at that. "I thought you liked Captain Underpants," she said.

I didn't answer.

"And last I checked," she went on, "you're not a baby. Or . . ." She tapped her chin. "Wait, did you start wearing a diaper without telling me?" She stuck her nose down near the seat of the chair I was sitting in and pretended to take a big sniff. "Do you need to be changed, Albie?"

I scooched my chair away from Calista's nose. Dad was right. That girl was off her rocker.

"I'm not wearing a diaper," I told her.

"So you're definitely not a baby, then," she said like she was thinking things through. "And you *do* like Captain Underpants." She tapped her chin again. "So one can only logically conclude"—*tap, tap, tap*—"that Captain Underpants is not for babies."

I sighed and reached for my backpack. "Mom wants me to read this book," I said, pulling out the stupid, long, boring book she'd given me. "But I tried, and the words don't make any sense."

"Ah," Calista said. She took the book and turned it over to look at the back. After a minute of reading, she said, "This looks awful."

"It is," I told her.

Calista thought while I buried my face on the table. I could tell she was thinking, because when she was done, she said, "Would your mom know if you didn't read this book? Why can't you go back to reading Captain Underpants? At least you like those books."

That surprised me when Calista said that, because it sounded like she was saying I should be sneaky and not tell my mom about Captain Underpants. Which is what I wanted to do anyway, but I was surprised about a grown-up saying it. Grown-ups weren't supposed to be sneaky.

"She'd see it on my reading log," I said. "And then she'd be mad all over again." I pressed my face harder into the table. Mrs. Rouse was getting mad about the reading log, so I knew I had to start reading something. But if I tried to read *Johnny Treeface* again, it would probably kill me. And I definitely didn't want to be dead from a book.

I didn't know what to do.

"It'll be all right, Albie," Calista said. "We'll figure something out. Now, why don't you go watch some TV?"

"But . . ." My fifteen minutes were already up. I was pretty sure Calista knew that, because she'd set the timer on the microwave herself.

"Albie," Calista said, and her voice was very serious, "I *insist* that you watch fifteen more minutes of television right this very second. Unless . . ." She tapped her chin again. "Did I hear you say you wanted to clean the toilet?"

"TV!" I said, laughing. "I pick TV!" And I raced for the couch before Calista could realize she was off her rocker again.

As soon as the timer on the microwave went off, Calista walked into the living room. I snapped off the TV. Calista was holding something behind her back, and I could tell she was up to something. I just couldn't tell what it was.

"What's that?" I asked, trying to peek.

Calista didn't answer. "You know," she said, "I started reading *Johnny Tremain,* and it turns out it's actually not so awful. Maybe you should try it again."

I wrinkled my nose. Is *that* what she was being sneaky about? "No, thanks," I said.

"All right," she said with a shrug. "It's up to you. But I think you might want to give it a shot. It looks like there are cartoons in it." And she tossed the book next to me on the couch and went back to the kitchen.

My head shot up. Cartoons? How come I hadn't noticed before that *Johnny Treeface* had cartoons in it? I turned to look at the book on the couch.

It wasn't *Johnny Treeface*. It was *Captain Underpants and the Perilous Plot of Professor Poopypants*, the same one I'd been reading before. Only Calista had made a new title for it, with construction paper and markers, and taped it to the front.

JOHNNY TREMAIN

by Esther Forbes

That's what it said on the front.

"Calista?" I called into the kitchen. I was staring at the book. "How come—?"

"After you're done reading," she called back, "be sure you spell the title right in your reading log, okay, Albie? *Johnny Tremain*. Just the one *e*."

I looked down at the book.

Johnny Tremain, that's what it said.

I smiled.

Then I opened the book, and I started to read.

being where you've been.

Normally we didn't have quizzes in math club, because it was a club not a class, but on Monday we had one. Mr. Clifton called it a "whiz quiz," to try to trick us into thinking it might be more fun than a regular quiz, I bet, but I was not tricked. It was all about multiplication, and I got almost all the answers wrong.

After math club was over, I stayed behind to tell Mr. Clifton something when nobody else was in the room.

"I don't think I should be in math club anymore," I told him.

Mr. Clifton set down the stack of papers he was holding. "Albie?" he said, like my name was a question. "Why would you want to drop out?"

"I just . . ." I scuffed my foot along the carpet. "I'm not very good at math. I think I . . ." I scuffed my foot some more, harder. "I don't think I should do any math anymore."

"Albie." That time my name was not a question.

Mr. Clifton didn't say anything after that, and I figured maybe he was waiting for me to look at him instead of at my shoes. So finally I did. Even though my shoes were more interesting.

"I want to show you something." That's what he said.

Mr. Clifton walked around behind his desk and pointed to something on the wall—a small blue piece of paper in a square black frame. I followed him so I could look at it more closely. I stood on my tiptoes and stuck my nose right close to the glass.

It was a report card.

NAME:	Daniel Clifton
GRADE:	4th
SCORES	
SCIENCE:	A
SOC. STUDIES:	B+
ART:	A-
READING:	A
MATH:	F

"That's *yours*?" I asked, settling down from my tiptoes.

"Yep," Mr. Clifton said.

"Mr. Clifton," I told him, very seriously, "you should probably take that down. Because otherwise someone might find out that you got an F in math."

Mr. Clifton just laughed at that, a real guffaw. "I keep it there on purpose," he said.

My eyes went wide. "You *do*?" That sounded crazy to me. Because why would anyone ever want to hang up an F report card, in a frame and everything? The worst report card I'd ever gotten from Mountford Prep had three U's for Unsatisfactory, and I threw that one down the garbage chute. I definitely didn't *frame* it.

"You can't get where you're going without being where you've been."

That's what Mr. Clifton said while I was still staring at his F report card.

"Huh?" That's what I said.

"My grandmother always used to tell me that," Mr. Clifton explained. "When I was a boy."

"Oh," I said.

I wonder if Mr. Clifton's grandmother ever saw that F report card.

"When I was a kid," Mr. Clifton said, "I hated math. *Hated* it. Because I was bad at it, and because I thought it didn't make any sense."

I nodded at that, because it was true. Math *didn't* make any sense.

"So that's why I decided to become a math teacher."

I stopped nodding when Mr. Clifton said that last part. Because *that* was a thing that didn't make any sense.

"What?" I said. "Why?"

He shrugged. "I figured if math didn't make any sense to me, it probably didn't make sense to lots of other people. So I promised myself that if I ever *did* figure it out, I'd become a math teacher so I could help other people who'd had trouble, just like me." He reached up and straightened the report card in its frame so it was exactly even to the ground. "It took a lot of hard work, but I'm glad every day that I made that decision and didn't end up with some super-easy profession, like neurosurgeon."

I just stared at him. Because I knew that Mr. Clifton liked to tell bad jokes, but this time I couldn't tell if he was joking. Who would actually *want* to be a math teacher?

"So I can't drop out of math club, then?" I asked.

"Not even a little," Mr. Clifton told me.

stacking cups.

Every time we went down to the bodega to get a donut, Calista always ended up talking to Hugo forever. That's because it turned out that Hugo liked art too. A lot. They would show each other sketches they were working on, and Calista would tell him stories about her art classes, and Hugo would laugh his big, growly old-man laugh.

At first I thought it was fun to listen to them, because it turns out Hugo is pretty interesting. I never knew that before when I just went there to buy donuts. I guess I never really thought about talking to him about art or anything.

But after a while, even art could get kind of boring. Plus I couldn't eat my donut until I'd paid for it, and so sometimes I was just standing there, staring at the donut in my hand for nine thousand years while I waited for Hugo to take my dollar, and my stomach would get rumbly.

So on Wednesday when we were there, I started stacking cups. Hugo's always doing it, taking the long stack of cups out of the plastic wrapper and sorting them into smaller stacks by the coffee pourers. I noticed him doing it all the time when we came in before. So on Wednesday I grabbed the stack that Hugo had set down when he started talking to Calista, and I started counting too.

Only I realized after I'd been counting for a while that I didn't know what I was supposed to be counting to.

"How many do you do?" I asked Hugo over my shoulder. Which I guess was interrupting, because he and Calista were looking at some boring art book he'd brought in to show her, but I didn't care.

"Sorry?" Hugo asked me.

"How many cups?" I asked. "What do I count to?"

Hugo straightened his back to get a better look at me from the counter. "Well, aren't you something?" he said, his eyes all smiles. "Thanks, Albie! I appreciate the help."

I stood there, waiting for him to tell me the number.

"I usually do about twenty-five cups in a stack," he told me.

When he said that, I had to start counting again, because I forgot what number I'd counted to already. But I finished the whole plastic row, four neat towers next to the sugar and the milk. They looked nice, I thought, all even like that.

"Thank you very much," Hugo said when I was done. "You're a wonderful helper."

"Isn't he great?" Calista said, and she mussed my hair. I didn't mind too much.

I put my strawberry glazed with rainbow sprinkles on the counter.

"On the house," Hugo told me.

I squinted at him.

"No charge," he said. "You help me stack, I give you donuts."

"Really?" I asked, staring at the donut sitting there on the counter. That seemed like a pretty good deal to me. "Can I help stack again tomorrow?"

Hugo laughed. "Any time, Albie."

And that's how I ended up with my new after-school job.

(not) johnny treeface.

When Mrs. Rouse was handing back our reading logs on Monday, she stopped at my desk and said she was very glad I was reading again.

I shrugged. I didn't want her to find out I was still reading baby books, even though on my reading log it said I was reading a book for a fifth-grader.

But I guess Mrs. Rouse is hard to trick, because she asked me, "How are you liking *Johnny Tremain*?"

It took me a second to remember that that was the real name of *Johnny Treeface*.

"It's, um, okay," I said slowly.

She smiled at me. "Glad to hear it," she told me. "I remember it being terribly boring. But I'm glad you're enjoying it." That's when I noticed her eyes darting down to my desk, where my copy of *Captain Underpants and the Wrath of the Wicked Wedgie Woman,* with Calista's fake cover, was sticking out. My stomach went hot, and I pushed the book in just a centimeter, but when I looked up at Mrs. Rouse, she was still smiling.

She winked at me.

"Keep it up, Albie," she said, and then she continued on down the row.

only
a test.

At dinner Mom told me that Ms. McPhillips, the school counselor, wanted me to take a test.

"What kind of a test?" I asked, because I hate tests. There is no such thing as a good test, unless maybe it's a test to figure out what is the very best kind of donut. But I've never taken that one.

"Oh, it's nothing to worry about," Mom said, which really made me start to worry, because that's exactly what she said when I had to get my cavity filled. "Ms. McPhillips thinks you might have a reading disorder, that's all."

I guess I must've made a face right then, and Mom figured out it was because of what she said, not the carrots I was eating (which were also awful). She put her hand on my arm, which was the arm holding my fork, which meant I couldn't eat any more carrots, which I was not that upset about.

"Albie," she said, "it's not a big deal. I promise."

"I don't have a disorder," I told her.

Then she told me about the thing Ms. McPhillips thought I might have in my brain, which was a long word I couldn't pronounce, with an *x* in it. "Lots of people have it, Albie," she said. "Famous people. Smart people. It just means your eyes mix up letters and numbers sometimes, and it would explain why you sometimes have trouble reading."

I put down my fork in my pile of gross carrots. "Lots of people have it?" I said.

Mom nodded. "And if *you* have it, then we need to know. You'd get extra time to take tests, extra help with your homework." She smiled. "We might finally get those grades of yours up. Wouldn't that be nice?"

I thought about that. Extra time on tests did sound sort of nice. Maybe I wasn't so bad at school after all. Maybe I was just one of those smart people like Mom was talking about who mixed up their numbers. "Yeah," I said.

Mom let me have ice cream even though I didn't finish all my carrots.

"Don't worry about it, okay?" she told me again as she flipped through the channels on the TV. I was curled up next to her on the couch, because Dad was working late, so he couldn't get mad about ice cream in the living room. "It's only a test."

But I could tell by the way Mom patted my leg with one hand as she watched the channels flick by that she wanted, more than anything, to find out that I had it. That big-word-*x* reading disorder.

I let my spoonful of cherry chunk ice cream melt into a tiny circle on my tongue. It was weird, I thought, knowing your mom wanted you to have a disorder. I always thought disorders were bad.

I scooped out another spoonful of ice cream.

I sort of hoped I had it too.

patience.

Patience is hard to have sometimes. Like with my A-10 Thunderbolt. Sometimes I couldn't wait for Dad to be home to help me, because I just wanted to work on the plane so bad. I wanted it to be a real whole Thunderbolt that flew, not just pieces in the box. So sometimes, when Dad wasn't home, I would take the pieces out of the box, out of their little plastic bags, and read the directions over and over and over and over until I could figure out where each tiny piece went. It was hard to tell a lot of times, because the directions were confusing, but if I stared and stared at the pictures, usually I could figure it out in the end. I'd mash the pieces right up next to each other, where they should go, and imagine what the plane would look like with everything finished. It would look exactly like the big A-10 Thunderbolt, the real one the air force pilots flew, that was at the Sea, Air, and Space Museum me and my dad went to one time.

A couple times I *really* didn't have patience, and I couldn't wait at all. I must've had ants in my pants like my mom said or something, but whatever the reason, I'd use the glue in the tiny bottle that came in the kit to glue some of the pieces in place. I was very careful with the bottle, to wipe down the tip with a wet paper towel when I was done and screw the lid on tight so no glue dried up. I always liked when new pieces of the plane were glued on permanently, because then I could start to see what it was going to look like. A real A-10 Thunderbolt. I must've been *super* bad at patience, because I did that a lot—gluing on pieces to see what they'd look like. Only sometimes. Only every now and then. When I got antsy pants waiting for Dad to help me. After I glued both wings on, the plane got too big to stick back in its box, so I had to hide it under a pillowcase on the top shelf in my closet. After that, I tried really hard to have better patience. Every once in a while, I would take the plane down and look at it, but I didn't add any more pieces, because I knew it would be more fun when Dad could help me. But I would look at it, and make it pretend zoom across my bedspread, and think about how after it was finished, me and Dad could put it on a display stand in the living room like Dad said. I really wanted to finish it. A year and a half was a long time to have patience. But I kept waiting. Because Dad said he wanted to help me build it, and I knew he'd be sad if I went ahead without him.

I could have patience for Dad.

friday.

W here can you find the most math teachers?" Mr. Clifton asked us on Friday, when we were all sitting down at our desks.

I thought hard, but I couldn't come up with the answer. No one else could either.

Mr. Clifton lowered his head to look at us above his glasses and then he told us the answer.

"*Math*-achusetts!"

We told him to use that one next year too.

the zombie
in the bathtub.

Mom said I should be Sherlock Holmes for Halloween again, but Calista had a way better idea.

A zombie.

"With ripped-up clothes and blood and everything?" I asked her when we were walking through the racks of kids' shirts at the Housing Works thrift shop. We'd taken the bus all the way up to 90th Street to get there. Calista said it was the best one, that they had all the best stuff for cheap. She also said that thrift stores were the best places to find Halloween costumes, but so far I didn't see anything that a zombie would wear. "I want it to look like I'm dead and all my guts are hanging out," I said. Calista nodded and held up a pair of pants to my legs, to see if they would fit, I guess. "And fangs. I want to have fangs."

"Zombies don't have fangs," Calista told me.

"Oh," I said, and I frowned. I'd really wanted to have fangs.

When Calista saw my face, she laughed. "You can be a fanged zombie if you want, Albie."

That made me smile.

My zombie outfit from the thrift store cost $7.85. Really it was just pants and a shirt—it didn't look like zombie clothes at all. But Calista said we could fix it so it did. After the thrift store, we went to Duane Reade and got a bottle of red hair dye, then we headed home.

"And now," Calista said while I swung the bags beside her, "we make magic."

It turned out that the way to make magic was to rip up my new thrift store clothes with a pair of scissors. Calista did most of the ripping.

"*Brains!*" I shouted while Calista ripped, because all zombies cared about was eating brains, and I needed to practice.

"Louder," Calista told me.

"*BRAINS!*" I shouted, louder.

"Much better."

I kept practicing while Calista showed me how to pour the dye over the clothes in the bathtub.

"*Brains! Mmm, brains!*"

Calista laughed.

It turned out zombies didn't just care about brains. One of the other things they *should* care about, according to Harriet, the cleaning lady who came once a week and who was about a million years old, was staining the bathtub. She came to clean while me and Calista were hanging the zombie clothes up in my room to dry, and we didn't realize she was there, actually, because she has her own key so she doesn't use the buzzer or anything, and all of a sudden, we heard all this *screaming* coming from the bathroom. And me and Calista ran-ran-ran down the hall from my bedroom, and when we were right outside the bathroom, Calista put a hand on my chest like she wanted me to stay in the hallway while she figured out what was going on. Only no way was I staying all by myself in the hallway if there was someone being *murdered* in our bathroom, which is what it sounded like, what with all the screaming and everything. So I ignored Calista's hand on my chest and peeked inside too.

It wasn't anybody being murdered. It was Harriet the cleaning lady, which I guess maybe I should've figured out.

Harriet looked up from the bathtub when she saw us— me and Calista in the doorway—and she stopped screaming that terrible scream, only her mouth was still open, so it looked like she might start up again any minute. And then she spent a few seconds looking back and forth between me and Calista and the bathtub, which was smeared with zombie blood. I was still holding the zombified shirt in my hand, and I finally realized that Harriet had been doing all that screaming because she thought *we'd* been murdered. And that was kind of funny, I thought, all of us thinking that someone else had been murdered, when really no one had been murdered at all. It had just been a Halloween zombie in the bathtub. Which was why I started laughing.

Harriet did not start laughing. She did not seem to think that zombies were very funny.

"I'm not cleaning that up," she told me. And then she stomped out of the bathroom and hollered at Calista if she knew where my parents kept the aspirin, and then she spent the next hour lying on the couch with a cool washcloth over her eyes while Calista and I scrubbed the tub clean.

But anyway, the zombie costume turned out pretty great.

a fresh piece
of paper.

When we finished with my homework on Wednesday, Calista said she wanted to do some drawing.

"What kind of drawing?" I asked.

"How about people?" she said. "Cartoons, maybe, like in *Captain Underpants*."

"Can we draw superheroes?" I asked. "I want to make my own superhero." I knew exactly the one I wanted to do.

"Sure," Calista said, so we got out the markers and paper.

Calista's superhero looked amazing. It was a girl superhero, and Calista named her Art Girl. She had curly hair and a paintbrush in one hand and one of those wooden things artist people put their thumbs through that has all the colors of paint on it. Also, she had a cape.

Calista said superheroes always had capes.

Calista sure was good at drawing. She was using the exact same markers as me, but somehow when she drew with them, her drawings looked a million times better than mine. My superhero was supposed to be Donut Man, the best superhero anybody ever invented. But he just looked like a blobby stick.

"What are you doing?" Calista asked when she looked over at me.

I had my head down on the table, close to her hand so I could watch while she drew, and my right hand was up in the air, gripped tight around the marker. "I'm trying to see if I'm holding it wrong," I said, but then I sat up, because all of a sudden I felt silly. "How come I can't draw as good as you?"

"Albie." Calista set down her marker and looked over at my paper. "Yours is good!"

It was not good. "That's what teachers say when they don't want to hurt your feelings," I told Calista. Then I grumped, crossing my hands over my chest. I was feeling particularly grumpy.

Calista glanced at me sideways. Then she leaned in close to look at my drawing a little harder. "All right," she said after a while. "It's awful."

At first that made me mad, because that was not the

thing a not-a-babysitter was supposed to say, especially a nice one. But when I saw the look on her face, a scrunched-up half smile, I couldn't help but laugh. Because Calista was telling the truth, and I knew it—my Donut Man drawing *was* awful.

"It's horrible!" I said, still laughing.

"Wretched!" Calista added.

"Gross!"

"Putrid!"

"Terrible!"

"An abomination!"

I shook my head. "I guess I'll never be an artist like you," I said.

Calista thought about that. "Oh, I don't know that *that's* true," she said. "I've had a lot more practice than you have. I could teach you a couple tricks, if you want."

"Really?"

"Sure."

So Calista took out a fresh piece of paper and gave me a new marker, one where the tip wasn't all mushed-up used. "We'll start easy," she said. And she drew one line, straight down the paper. She told me to draw one just like it, right beside it. So I did. I copied her like that, one little step after another, and when we were done and we pulled our hands from the paper, wouldn't you know it—Calista had shown me how to draw a whole person. Head, legs, feet, every-thing. It wasn't a superhero yet, just a person. Actually it was a little bit like a stick figure, like in hangman, but with more details. Then Calista showed me how to make changes, whatever I wanted, like giving the man muscles or a fat belly, or bending his arms or making him run, or anything. By dinnertime we had tons of people, all different kinds, crammed all up and down and sideways across the paper. I'd even drawn a better version of Donut Man.

He looked pretty okay.

"See?" Calista said as she got up to put water on for spaghetti. "I told you you could do it."

I looked down at the paper. You could tell which people were Calista's and which ones were mine, because Calista's were better. But mine weren't *awful*.

"Do you think I could ever get good enough to be an artist one day?" I asked Calista as she turned the heat on under the pot on the stove.

"I don't know," Calista said. "Do you want to be an artist?"

I looked at Donut Man some more. For a long time. "I want to be something I'm good at," I said.

"Albie."

Calista walked over and leaned her elbows on the counter by the table. I looked up at her. She looked more serious than normal. "You should do something because you *love* it, not just because you're good at it."

I wrinkled my nose, thinking. "But you're good at art, and you love it," I told her.

She nodded. "Did you ever think maybe the love part comes first?" I guess she could tell I was confused, because she kept talking. "Find something you'd want to keep doing forever," she said, "even if you stink at it. And then if you're lucky, with lots of practice, then one day you won't stink so much."

That sounded good. But . . .

"But what if I'm not lucky?" I asked her. "What if I *do* find something I love, and then I always just stink at it?"

Calista smiled her thoughtful smile. "Then won't you be glad you found something you love?" she said.

And I didn't really get a chance to answer, because then she said, "I'm too hungry to wait for the spaghetti to boil. What do you say we eat cookies first?"

That was one thing I didn't have to think about too hard. Even if they weren't nearly as good as donuts, I *knew* I loved cookies.

the thing about the cups.

Here's what I figured out about the coffee cups at the bodega downstairs that I stacked after school for free donuts while Calista was looking at art books with Hugo.

I always ended up with four stacks of them. Always. Every single time. Twenty-five cups in each stack. One, two, three, four.

I looked on the plastic bag once, and it said ONE HUNDRED PAPER CUPS.

That's how I knew that there were four stacks of twenty-five in one hundred. Every time.

Here's another thing I figured out. Once I'd counted out three stacks—one, two, three—then I didn't have to count the last one. Because no matter what, it would be twenty-five in the stack, every single time.

I figured that out by myself. No one told me.

I told that to Mr. Clifton, because he asked me what I liked to do after school, so I told him, and he grinned at me and said, "Albie, I think you accidentally did math."

"Really?" I asked. I almost didn't believe it.

He nodded. "Did it hurt?" he said.

I thought about that. Usually math hurt my brain, like a tree crashing down inside it over and over. But this time it didn't hurt at all.

"Nope," I said.

Mr. Clifton gave me a high five.

I hoped I could accidentally do math some more. It turned out that was the best way to do it.

change
of plans.

There was a storm on Halloween. A big one. So big that Erlan's family couldn't go to the Halloween Parade in the Village like they'd been planning, because all the camera equipment might get soaked.

"Too bad," Erlan said. But I could tell he wasn't really upset about it.

So that was the good part—that Erlan couldn't go to the Halloween Parade and instead got to go trick-or-treating with me and Betsy.

The bad part was that the storm was so terrible that

Mom called from work and said she was going to be late getting home, because of the subway being flooded. She also said that she didn't think we should go out trick-or-treating on Columbus Avenue like we always did.

"Buh they hah the bess candy!" I shouted into the phone. I was already dressed up in my zombie costume—Calista had even put some gross scabby makeup on my face before she went home—and I knew I sounded like a baby, but I didn't care. I popped my zombie fangs out of my mouth so I could talk better. "That's where we go every year."

On the couch, Betsy looked down at her boots. She was dressed like a rock climber, with a rope around her waist and a headlamp and everything. She was pretending not to listen to me on the phone, but I knew she really heard. Erlan was listening too. He was dressed like a pirate, with an eye patch and a fake stuffed parrot elasticked to his arm.

"Your father can take you trick-or-treating in the building," Mom said. "Plenty of our neighbors will be handing out candy. Put your dad on, okay?"

I didn't want to, but I did.

After that, I was sure Halloween was going to be awful, but it turned out it wasn't. I was sure Dad wouldn't wear a costume to help us trick-or-treat, but it turned out I was wrong about that too. Even if I didn't get what it was he was supposed to be.

"I'm a pencil pusher," he told us, stretching out the cup

of pencils in his hand in front of him again, like that would make it make more sense.

Betsy giggled, but Erlan just said, "Huh?" which was what I was thinking. I didn't really care what Dad's costume was, though, as long as I got candy.

We went trick-or-treating all over our building, starting on the first floor and going door to door, to every apartment with a pumpkin sticker outside. We zoomed up the stairs because that was faster than the elevator. *Tons* of people had candy. There were tons of other kids too, from all over the building. Some of them I'd never even seen before. Everyone loved my zombie costume and said how great and scary it was. *"Brains!"* I told them, which meant "thank you" in Zombie. Erlan started shouting *"brains!"* too, even though that's not what pirates say. And Betsy said "trick or treat" twice with no stuttering. I heard her.

We trick-or-treated for over an hour, even after the lights went out when we were on the ninth floor. Betsy lit the way with her rock-climbing headlamp, and people opened their doors holding candles. And one guy said he didn't figure he'd see any more kids the whole rest of the night because of the power, so he dumped his whole bowl of candy between our three bags and told us, "Enjoy!"

The whole bowl!

After the trick-or-treating, we went back to our apartment, and we sat on the floor with candles all around and split up our candy. Betsy and me loved loved loved chocolate, but Erlan wanted mostly fruit candies, so that was good for splitting. There were lots of Smarties, and Erlan got a record-high *nine*-Smarties tower on his tongue before Betsy made him laugh and they all spilled on the carpet. Dad couldn't do any work on his computer because of the power being out, so he stayed in the living room, not in his office. And when Mom finally got home, dripping and soaking from having to walk the whole way from her office in the storm, she let us eat on the floor, on a blanket, like a picnic. We had macaroni and cheese—the kind from the box that was only for weekends—and Mom put some peas in it because "at least we can *pretend* to be healthy." And when we were done with dinner, we told ghost stories, even Dad, and Betsy kept screaming and hiding her face in her sweatshirt, but she was laughing too, so I think she was having fun.

Betsy had to spend the night, since her parents couldn't come get her because of the subway. Erlan could've gone home, obviously, since he was right across the hall, but his parents said he could spend the night if he wanted. I'd never had a Tuesday-night sleepover before. This was turning into the best Halloween ever.

We were rolling out the sleeping bags and blankets on the floor in the living room when Betsy whispered to me, "Hey, Alb-Albie?"

"Yeah?" I said. Erlan was in the bathroom changing into his pajamas, so it was just me and Betsy in the living room.

I tossed a pillow up at the top of the sleeping bag, where my head would go.

Betsy tucked her chin into the T-shirt Mom gave her to wear as a pajama top. She was wearing a pair of my old pajama pants on bottom, the dog ones. She squeezed a pillow to her chest and looked up at me.

"This is f-fun," she told me. She didn't say anything else, because that was right when Erlan came back into the living room and so she got shy again, but I could tell by the look on her face what she was thinking. I would bet a million dollars that she was thinking that she wished every day could be Halloween.

That was what I was thinking too.

gus.

Calista did have a boyfriend. His name was Gus. I found that out when I asked her about the neon pink streak in her hair, which sometimes you could see if her hair was in braids, but most of the time you couldn't. When I asked her about it, Calista said, "Oh, do you like it? I'm thinking of getting rid of it because Gus says he hates it." And I said, "Who's Gus?" even though I thought I probably knew already. And she said, "My boyfriend. Didn't I tell you about him?" And I said, "No," and then she told me all about him, even though I didn't say I wanted to know.

Gus was twenty-four, which was three years older than Calista.

He was from California, just like Calista. They went to high school together. But they didn't start dating till a year ago.

Gus could've been the valedictorian of their school, because he was so smart. But he never was the valedictorian. Calista didn't say why.

She also didn't tell me what a valedictorian was, but lucky for me, I didn't care.

Gus didn't think Calista should've gone to art school. Calista seemed mad about that, even though she laughed when she told me.

Gus moved to New York City to be an actor, because he was very talented. When I asked what movies he had been in, Calista said, "Well, not much yet. But he goes to lots of auditions."

I had a nanny once who went to lots of auditions. She moved to Michigan to be a kindergarten teacher.

"Do you want to see a picture of him?" Calista asked me. "I'll show you on my phone."

"No, thanks," I told her. "I'll wait till he's in a movie."

Maybe Gus would move to Michigan too.

parent-
teacher
conferences.

Parent-teacher conferences were on Monday. Mom went. Dad too. I had sort of forgotten they were going, but when they came home, I remembered.

Dad did not look happy.

"Albie, these grades are unacceptable," he said, throwing a stack of papers on the table. My grades or homework or something, I guess. I didn't look.

"Richard, please," my mom said. But she didn't say please what. She dug some money out of her wallet and handed it to Calista.

"Bye, Albie," Calista said softly before she snuck out the door.

I wished I could sneak out the door.

"You have a D in spelling," Dad told me before the door was even closed. "A *D*. How hard is it to spell a couple words?"

"Richard," Mom said.

"I study every Thursday," I said. My voice was so soft even I could barely hear it. "Calista helps me. We make flash cards. The problem is Mrs. Rouse picks new words every week."

"Well, perhaps you should study every *Wednesday* too," Dad said. "And Tuesday and Monday. D's are not okay in this house, Albie."

Mom sighed, but she didn't say anything. She went into the kitchen and opened the fridge.

She didn't take anything out.

"I expect you to get a perfect score on your next spelling test, Albie."

"Perfect?" I said. "But that's ten whole words!" How could I get ten right when I could barely get four?

"It's not up for debate, Albie. Any son of mine should be able to spell. Do better."

After Dad left the room, Mom closed the fridge and looked at me sitting at the table.

"Time to get ready for bed, okay, Albie?" she said.

I went to my room and changed into my pajamas, even though I hadn't taken my shower yet. But no one seemed to notice.

I hated parent-teacher conferences.

studying.

I started studying for my spelling test the very next day, Tuesday, which was two days before I normally started.

"Well, aren't you the model student?" Calista said when I told her I wanted to make flash cards early.

Simple. S-I-M-P-L-E. That one was simple. "Rhymes with *pimple,*" Calista said while we drew pictures on the back of the flash card. That made me laugh.

Brain. B-R-A-I-N. That one was a little harder, because there were so many ways to make the long-*a* sound. "Albie has good grades on the *b-r-a-i-n,*" Calista said.

Especially. E-S-P-E-C-I-A-L-L-Y. That one was impossible. "*Especially* is an especially stupid spelling word," I said.

We studied and studied and studied.

And the more we studied, the more I knew I'd never be able to get all ten right. No matter how hard I tried, I wasn't ever going to be a perfect speller.

I wondered how such a perfect speller like Dad could end up with a son like me.

what's wrong with my brain.

A s soon as Mom hung up the phone with the counselor, I could tell something was wrong. Her eyebrows
were all crinkly.

"What?" I asked her.

Mom didn't look at me. She set her phone down on a
stack of papers and opened up the cupboard with the
mugs. "That was Ms. McPhillips," she said, and she peered
inside one of the mugs like there was something dirty in it,
then put it in the sink. She took out another one. "With the
results of the test you took last week."

"Oh." As soon as she said that, I knew it was something

real bad. "Did I do something wrong?" I asked. I was always screwing up on tests.

"Oh, Albie, no," she said, setting the mug on the counter. But she still didn't look at me. She was searching through another cupboard now, the one with tea and rice and stuff. I thought if she was really mad at me for screwing up the test super bad, she'd probably be yelling at me, but I was confused too because when I do good on tests, she always gave me a big hug and told me how proud she was. And she wasn't doing either of those things.

"It's not bad," she went on. Which made me let out a little breath I didn't know I was holding. "It's . . . ," she said. But then she paused for a second, searching through all the teas in the cupboard—picking them up and then setting them down in different stacks. "You don't have dyslexia," she said at last.

"Dis-what?" I asked.

"*Dyslexia,* Albie," she said, and that time she did sound like she was mad at me, although I couldn't tell why. "The reading disorder Ms. McPhillips tested you for. Remember?"

I wanted to say that of course I remembered. I was the one who took it. But Mom was mad, and I didn't know why, and I didn't want to make her madder. "I don't have it?" I asked.

She shifted another box of tea to look behind it. "No," she said.

"So I did good on the test?"

"It's *well,* Albie," she said, slamming the box of tea down.

Maybe she was mad at the tea. "You did *well*. And it's not a matter of—" She stopped talking and set the mug down on the counter. She closed the cupboard with a soft click. "You do not have a reading disorder," she said, looking up at me. "That's the important thing."

"Oh," I said again. All of a sudden my insides felt twisted, like I wasn't sure whether I should be happy or sad. Because it seemed like it should be a good thing, that I didn't have that long-word-*x* reading disorder, that my brain didn't mix up letters and numbers on the page. But I could tell from the look on Mom's face that she didn't think it was.

"Maybe I can take the test again," I said quietly.

Mom closed her eyes for a long time, not talking, and after a while, I started to worry that maybe she had fallen asleep like that, standing up, and that maybe I should try to shake her or something. But then she opened her eyes and said, "Your father forgot to get coffee. I'm going to run downstairs to get some. I'll be back in a sec, okay?" And she grabbed her purse and her keys, gave me a peck on the forehead, and left me at the table with my social studies homework.

The whole time she was gone, I stared at the page and squinted and shifted my head to look at it, but no matter which way I turned—me or the paper—I couldn't get the letters to look funny. The *d* was just a *d*. The *p* was just a *p*. And even when I blinked, faster faster faster, *bad* didn't come out looking like *dab*. I shoved the paper in my backpack and gave up trying. I was never going to get a reading disorder.

When Mom came back, she put the coffee in the cupboard but left her mug on the counter and said she needed to lie down for a bit. I didn't tell her that we already had coffee, that Dad had told her yesterday that he wanted to start keeping it in the freezer for freshness. I didn't tell her that. I didn't say anything. Because nothing I thought mattered. And I had a test to prove it.

The only thing wrong with my brain was my brain.

things
i don't know.

I don't know how to spell "mountain." Or "business." Or "especially." I do the flash cards over and over, and I never get those ones right.

I don't know how to subtract without a pencil.

I don't know Mom's cell phone number without looking it up, even though I call it all the time.

I don't know the name of Dad's company he works for. I stopped asking because he rolls his eyes every time I ask and says, "Albie, I *told* you." But I never remember.

I don't know how many nickels in a dollar, or how many

dimes. Darren Ackleman says everybody learned that in first grade. Somehow I didn't.

I don't know the capital of Arkansas, and I don't care. Arkansas should go learn its own capital.

I don't know the best way to make a model volcano, or what it feels like to get your Science Fair project picked to go to the gym for Parents' Night.

I don't know how *anybody* could like *Johnny Tremain*.

I don't know how to make my dad smile when he looks at my report card, instead of clenching his jaw tight.

I don't know how to make Mom stop worrying so much about me, even though she says she doesn't.

I don't know why I'm always screwing up at everything, even when I try so hard, all the time, not to. I'd do better if I could, I really would. But I don't know how.

There are a lot of things I don't know.

donut
days.

Thursday night, me and Calista studied and studied with the flash cards.

Five, that was the most words I could get right at once.

Five was not perfect.

After I took a shower and was in my pajamas, I told Calista I was coming down with the flu, but I could tell she didn't believe me.

"You didn't have the flu thirty minutes ago, when we were eating dinner."

"It came on all of a sudden," I explained.

"Mmm-hmm." She crinkled her mouth up and peeled the *Johnny Tremain* title off the old *Captain Underpants* I already finished and stuck it to the new one. "This flu wouldn't have anything to do with your spelling test tomorrow, would it?"

I shook my head. "I feel really sick," I said. Which was true. Every time I thought about that spelling test and not getting all ten words 100 percent perfect, I felt sick, right in my stomach. It would be better if I just stayed home.

She put her hand on my forehead. "You're not warm," she said slowly. She studied my face carefully. "Well, I guess we'll know if you're really sick if you start to feel sharp pains on the left side in your ribs. That's usually the first sign of the flu."

I was just moving my hand over to see if I had sharp pains there, where Calista said, when I saw the look on her face, and I stopped. "Is that really true?" I asked her.

She rolled her eyes. "No," she told me.

I moved my hand away. "Then my ribs don't hurt at all."

"Albie." Calista sat down on the bed and patted the bedspread for me to sit down next to her. I sat. She looked at me for a long time, but she didn't say anything. Which was weird. Then she got up and left the room. I stayed put. I didn't know what else to do.

When Calista came back, she was carrying her blue backpack. She sat back down and pulled out a handful of papers, all sorts. Some on thick paper and some that looked like they were ripped out of her sketchbook, because they had crinkled edges on the side. She looked through them and then handed me one.

I looked at it carefully. It was covered in drawings, all of them done with a pencil. They were all of people—some sitting up, some standing, some lying down. They looked realistic, not like the cartoon people she was helping me draw. Lots of them were just parts, elbows floating next to a pair of crossed legs and, next to that, three pairs of feet. Hands were everywhere—open, holding pencils, scrunched up like a fist. Some of the pictures were scribbled over, like they were started and then given up halfway through.

"You did these?" I asked Calista.

She nodded, but she was still flipping through her mess of papers. "For my figure drawing class," she said. She glanced over at the paper in my hands. "Look," she told me. "Right there." She tapped a bright blue sticky note stuck to the top of the paper. "That's from my teacher, Professor Milton."

I read what was on the sticky note.

Lacks perspective

I didn't know what that meant, but I could tell by the way Calista had her mouth scrunched up while she looked at it that it wasn't a good thing.

"Here's another one."

She handed me another paper of sketches. The sticky note on top of that one said *Blocky*. Calista gave me another paper, then another after that, and another and another. They all had sticky notes on them.

> *Loose lines*
> *No movement*
> *Stiff!*
> *Draw what you SEE*
> *Are you even trying?*

"I hate Professor Milton," Calista told me when I was finished reading all the sticky notes.

I looked up at her. "You do?" That surprised me, I guess, because I couldn't really imagine Calista hating anything. But I thought I might hate someone, too, if they wrote sticky notes like that to me.

"Yep," she said. "But I still go to class, every week, because I have to."

I was starting to see where this was going. "And you don't ever get the flu?" I asked her. I was pretty sure I already knew the answer, though.

She shook her head. "You know what I do instead?" I didn't answer, because I didn't know what she did. "I found a soft-serve place," she said, "right by the school. Tasti D-Lite, the one you told me about, remember?" I remembered. "And I tell myself that every Tuesday afternoon, after class is over, I get to stop there and have some ice cream."

"With sprinkles?" I asked, because I knew that Calista liked sprinkles.

"*Lots* of sprinkles," she said.

"That doesn't sound too bad."

"Right? So now, when I wake up on Tuesday mornings, instead of thinking, 'Ugh, I have to go to Professor Milton's class today,' I try to think, 'Hey, I get ice cream after class today!'"

I squinted one eye at her. "And that works?" I asked. "You never feel like getting the flu?"

Calista nodded. "Most of the time I don't."

I thought about that. "Can tomorrow be an ice cream day for me?" I asked.

Calista handed me *Johnny-Treeface*-not-*Captain-Underpants*. "I think it needs to be."

"Okay," I said. "But instead of ice cream, can it be donuts? Because I like donuts better."

"I'll make sure we get some when I pick you up," she said.

"Can we go to the bakery on Seventy-Eighth Street? They have the best donuts. Even better than the ones at the bodega."

"Sounds perfect."

"But it's all the way on up Seventy-Eighth Street, though. That's far."

"Not too far for Donut Day. Now get some sleep, all right, Albie? Good night."

"Night, Calista."

Donuts, I thought, after I was done with my reading and turned off my lamp. *Donuts.* Every once in a while, the spelling test would sneak back into my brain, but mostly Calista was right. It was way better to look forward to a donut day than a spelling test.

afterward.

The spelling test went okay. I wouldn't find out my grade until Monday, but I thought I got more than four. Maybe I even got perfect.

Calista let me get a chocolate donut *and* a jelly-filled from the bakery on 78th Street. They were good. Almost worth having a spelling test for.

Almost.

monday.

On Monday Mr. Clifton's joke was "Who's the king of the pencil case?" And the answer was "The ruler!" No one laughed at that one.

"You can do better than that, Mr. Clifton," Savannah told him.

And that made *Mr. Clifton* laugh.

I guess he won't be using that one again next year.

six words.

I got six words right on my spelling test. Six whole words. That was more than I ever got before. I even got *especially*. E-S-P-E-C-I-A-L-L-Y.

Language. That was one I missed, because I mixed up the *u* and the *a*. "That's a tough one," Calista told me after she high-fived me for my six whole words. "I even spell that one wrong sometimes." Which I knew was probably a lie, but I let her say it anyway.

Soccer. That was another one I didn't get. *Soccer* was supposed to be an easy one, but I forgot about the *-er* not *-re* at the end. I got confused and screwed up. "Sometimes it's the easy ones that get you," Calista said.

Calista took me to the bodega and told Hugo about my six words, and he was so impressed with me he gave me a giant bear claw that I didn't even have to stack cups for. I stacked cups anyway, though. I stacked a whole bunch of cardboard coffee sleeves too.

Hugo and Calista were talking awhile.

I couldn't decide if I was happy about the six words or not. Because for one thing, six words was good. I'd never gotten six whole words before. But for the other thing, six words wasn't perfect. It wasn't even almost. And Dad said I better get perfect.

My stomach was tied up like knots on a rope waiting for Dad to get home, to see what he'd say about the six words when I told him. But when he got home, he didn't ask about my spelling test. So I didn't tell him. He didn't ask the whole rest of the week either. I think maybe he forgot.

I couldn't decide if I was happy about that or not.

crying.

Calista was acting funny when she picked me up from school. Quiet. Sniffly. And she forgot which street I lived on too, and I knew she knew that one.

"You were crying," I told her once I figured it out. "Before you picked me up."

"No, I wasn't," she said. But I knew what crying looked like.

I knew what it sounded like too. I heard her when she went into the bathroom when we got home. She said she had to pee, but that was a lie too, because I heard her on the phone. She was trying to whisper, I think, but if that was true, then she wasn't doing a very good job. I couldn't hear any words, just angry talking, but then all of a sudden, I did hear some words. Five of them.

"Gus, just *listen* all right?"

So that's how I figured out she was talking to Gus.

"You're being a real idiot."

That was five more words I heard.

It sounded like it got angrier after that, the talking, but I didn't try to hear any more of the words. I went and sat on the couch in the living room.

I didn't know anything about that Gus, but I did know that if Calista was yelling-whispering at him in the bathroom when she said she had to pee, then he probably wasn't very nice. Nice people didn't make other people yell-whisper instead of pee.

Anyway, I didn't like him. I decided Calista was right. Gus *was* an idiot. Then I started to wonder how come someone so smart like Calista would have a boyfriend who was a real idiot. But I must not be very good at figuring, because that one just didn't make sense to me.

superheroes.

So what's Donut Man's superpower, anyway?" Calista asked when she was showing me some more art tricks on Thursday, after we both got sick of studying spelling flash cards. "Eating donuts?" She scratched her nose with the end of her marker. "Making donuts?"

I shook my head. "He doesn't have a superpower. He just really likes donuts."

"But he's a *superhero*," Calista said. "That means he *has* to have a superpower."

"Nope," I said, because I was pretty sure she was wrong.

"Some people aren't good at anything. Some people just really like donuts."

Calista looked at me for a long time, her marker raised in the air, and she didn't say anything. She didn't really even move. She sat there like that for so long that I started to worry that maybe her marker was going to dry out, because the cap was off. But finally she blinked and looked down at her paper and said, "Okay, Albie. Here, I'll show you how to do feet."

"Thanks," I told her.

just like me.

Mom likes to go through the papers in my take-home folder every night if she doesn't get home too late. I try to keep them neat, but sometimes I forget and smush them.

"Albie!" she said when she was looking through the folder. It was a really excited "Albie!" so for a second, I thought she was going to say how proud she was of me doing such good reading with *Johnny Treeface* (even though it wasn't really *Johnny Treeface*, it was really three different

Captain Underpants books, but she didn't know that). But anyway, that's not what she was "Albie!"-ing about.

"What?" I asked, trying to sneak a peek around her arm. "What is it?"

She put my take-home folder on the table. "You never told me you were having class elections," she said. I knew she was smiling even before I looked at her face, that's how excited she sounded. "What are you going to run for?"

I pressed the two twenty-dollar bills for the Chinese food on the table into a neat stack so they were one right on top of the other.

"I'm not running for anything," I told Mom. "Mrs. Rouse said we didn't have to. It's only if we want."

"You know," Mom said, pulling the page out of the folder and settling into a chair, "I was treasurer of my tenth-grade class. I beat out five other students." She seemed very happy about that.

I put the top twenty on the bottom and re-neatened the stack. I wondered when the doorbell would ring already, because Mom had called at least twenty minutes ago and I was getting pretty hungry. Usually the delivery people were super quick.

"Well, it's not real elections," I said. "Just fifth grade. It's stupid anyway. The president takes attendance, and the vice president turns the lights on and off. Stupid stuff like that." The hall manager was in charge of the bathroom pass. Being in charge of the bathroom pass sounded like the grossest job in the whole world.

"You have to start somewhere, right?" Mom said. "This could be good practice for when you want to run in high school. When do you have to decide by?"

"Two weeks. But I already decided I don't want to."

Mom shook her head and stuck the paper back in my folder without even looking at all the good reading in my reading log. "Don't be such a party pooper, Albie. Who knows? Maybe you'll end up being treasurer just like me, huh?"

When the food came, Wei frowned at me when I asked for the change, and he didn't say *shee-shee* either. He stood in the door for a long time and didn't leave until I said good-bye. Which I thought was weird, because usually Wei was so friendly. But then while we were eating, I started to get a sour feeling in my stomach, and when Mom got up for more water, I did math with a pencil on my napkin, and I realized I only tipped Wei sixty cents.

I was pretty sure I would never end up treasurer of anything.

thursday.

On Thursday Mr. Clifton raised his eyebrows at all of us and said, "If you had two tennis balls in your left pocket and seven tennis balls in your right pocket, what would you have?"

We all sort of shuffled around in our seats and didn't say anything. I didn't know what everyone else was thinking, but *I* was thinking that this was supposed to be joke time, so why was Mr. Clifton trying to make us do math? I wasn't too happy about it either.

But then Mr. Clifton lowered his head and looked at us over the top of his glasses and said, "You'd have . . . *really big pockets!*" And just like that, the room pretty much exploded with laughing. I was giggling so hard I almost fell out of my chair. Even Savannah was laughing, so I knew it was a good one.

friends.

On Saturday when I was at the park with Erlan and his brothers and sisters and two of their nannies, I saw Darren Ackleman throwing a football with his dad. Me and Erlan were playing poker on the bench while the other kids ran around screaming. The cameras were everywhere, but they couldn't film me because I was "no release!" I think that made Erlan happy, because it meant they mostly stayed away from our card game.

"That's him," I whispered to Erlan. "That mean kid from my school. Darren. With the bug."

Erlan lifted his head and turned to look behind him at Darren with his dad across the grass. He sort of showed me his cards when he did it, but I tried not to look, because that would be cheating.

Next to us on the bench, Calista looked up to see Darren too, but she didn't say anything about him, just went back to drawing in her sketchbook.

"That kid with the football?" Erlan asked, turning back to look at me.

"Yeah," I said.

"He looks like he smells."

I laughed. Darren didn't smell, not really, but I liked that Erlan thought he might.

"I raise you three acorns," I said.

After Erlan and his family had to go home and the whole camera crew left too, Calista and I decided to stay in the park and play cards a little longer, because it was a nice day outside, and also because Dad was home and he had a bad headache and said he didn't want to be bothered by anything. Calista said the best way not to bother anybody was to stay in the park. So we stayed.

Calista was teaching me a new card game called Spit, where you had to slap your cards down really fast. I was good at it, faster than Calista most times. Only sometimes I'd get *too* fast and my cards would fall between the slats of the bench onto the ground, and then we had to make the game pause while I picked them up.

I'd just won my third game in a row when all of a sudden I heard, "Hey, Albie." I looked up, and Darren Ackleman was standing right next to me.

I waited for Darren to say something mean, but he didn't.

"How's it going?" That's what he said.

I looked over at Calista, but she wasn't paying any attention. She was just shuffling the deck of cards, over and over. I didn't know you had to shuffle them that much, but I guess so.

"Pretty good," I told Darren, which was true.

Darren stuck his hands in his pockets. "How come all the cameras were here?" he asked. "Were they making a movie?"

Calista's shuffling got really loud, and she started cracking the cards on the bench between shuffles. But she still wasn't paying any attention to us.

I shook my head at Darren, to answer his question about the movie. "It's for my friend Erlan's family," I told him. It was weird because Darren wasn't being mean to me like he normally was at school. So I decided not to be mean back. "They're making a reality show."

Darren's eyes got all big. "Really?" he said. "Cool! And you're friends with him?"

Calista's shuffling got so loud that it made a squirrel jump into a nearby trash can.

"Yeah," I told Darren. "Erlan's been my best friend since six years ago. He lives on my floor. He's really cool. He likes chess." I don't know why I said that last part.

"Wow," Darren said. He seemed impressed. I guess it was sort of impressive, that I had a really cool best friend who likes chess.

Darren took his hands out of his pockets and then stuck them back in. "Hey, you want to play football with me and my dad?" he asked.

I looked at Calista, and she shrugged, still shuffling her cards. "It's up to you, Albie," she said. So I went.

It turned out Darren wasn't mean like I thought. Actually, it turned out he was really friendly. His dad too. Darren's dad taught me all sorts of useful stuff, like the right way to hold the football and how to throw it so it spiraled just right. I wasn't very good at that stuff, but Darren's dad said I had potential.

Calista stayed on the bench with her sketchbook the whole time. I guess she didn't like football. I noticed she kept watching us, though.

I told Darren's dad that I thought the bug Darren brought in for Science Friday was super cool, and he laughed and said that if I liked *that* one, I should come over someday after school with Darren and see his whole collection.

"Really?" I said. I turned to Darren.

"Yeah, totally," Darren told me. He was smiling. "That would be cool. You should bring your friend too."

"Betsy?" I said. I didn't know Darren liked Betsy. But I didn't know that Darren liked *me* before that day either, so I guess sometimes you can just be wrong about things. "I'm not sure if she could come." She liked bugs, but she didn't like Darren. I was pretty sure about that one.

"No," Darren said. "Your other friend. Erlan."

"Oh," I said. "Okay."

"Bugs aren't for girls," Darren said. And I don't know why, but I nodded at that like I thought it was true, even though I didn't.

I was almost 100 percent sure that Erlan thought bugs were gross.

"Well, champ," Darren's dad said, putting a hand on my shoulder. I liked being called "champ." No one had ever called me that before. "We better get going. It was nice meeting you."

"You too, Mr. Ackleman," I said. "Thanks for teaching me about football."

Darren put out his fist like he wanted to fist-bump me, so I fist-bumped. Darren had pointy knuckles. "Stay cool, Albie," he said. "See you Monday!"

And when Darren and his dad were walking away, I heard his dad say, "That's a very nice friend you've got there, Darren."

A friend. Darren Ackleman was my friend, and I didn't even know it.

"You have fun?" Calista asked me when I got back to the bench. She had all our stuff packed up, ready to go home.

"Yeah," I said. "Darren and his dad are pretty nice."

Calista raised her eyebrows at me like she wanted to say

something, but she didn't. She just hoisted the backpack onto her shoulder.

"What?" I asked. Because I was wondering what it was she didn't want to tell me.

"Just . . ." Calista was staring off across the grass. Finally she looked back at me. "Just be careful, all right?"

"Be careful of what?" I said. I didn't see anything to be careful of, like a dog that wanted to bite me or a mud puddle to slip in or anything.

Calista handed me the trash from our snack and we headed off down the path back to my building.

"Sometimes," Calista said slowly, and then she stopped to point to the garbage can, and I threw the trash inside. "Sometimes people aren't always nice for good reasons."

That made me confused. Because how could being nice not be good? And then I got even more confused, because I figured out that she was probably talking about Darren.

"But he's my friend," I told her. His dad had even said so. "And he said I was cool."

Calista sighed. "I just don't want to see you get hurt, Albie, that's all. Promise me you'll be careful around that kid."

"I promise," I told Calista, because I could tell she was upset, and I didn't like when she was upset. But I wasn't really sure what I was promising, because what did she mean about being careful? And anyway, she was just being silly. No way Darren would ever *hurt* me.

That wasn't the kind of thing friends did.

isn't.

Dad remembered about the spelling. Three weeks after the parent-teacher conference, he asked me how I'd been doing with my grades. So I showed him the last one.

Seven. Seven words. The best I'd ever done. Calista gave me two whole chocolate donuts after I showed her.

But I knew by the look on Dad's face when he saw that C grade at the top that I wasn't getting any donuts from him.

"I only missed three words," I told him. My voice was a squeak. "That's seven right. Which is almost all of them."

"Almost, Albie," Dad said slowly, putting the test down on the table, "isn't nearly good enough."

being cool.

ere's what it's like to be cool:

Cool kids play Pokémon by the drinking fountains before school starts. I found that out on Monday when I got to school. Darren saw me walking up the steps and pulled me over. I never knew that the cool kids did that before. No one told me. I always thought drinking fountains were just for drinking.

Cool kids don't raise their hands to answer questions in class. That's what Darren told me. I liked that rule, because I hardly ever know the answer to Mrs. Rouse's questions anyway. Maybe I was cool all along, and I never realized it.

At recess the cool kids play tetherball, which it turns out I'm sort of okay at.

The only thing I didn't like about being cool was that I couldn't sit next to Betsy at lunch because Darren said cool kids didn't sit next to kids who weren't cool, and Darren said Betsy definitely wasn't cool.

"Maybe she *is* cool," I said when we were all grabbing our lunches from our cubbies. Betsy was frowning at me talking to Darren, and I didn't like it. "She never raises her hand in class either."

Darren snorted. "Buh-Buh-Buh-Betsy," he said, "is *not* cool."

I was starting to think I didn't get what was cool and what wasn't.

I told Darren I needed to talk to Mrs. Rouse about something, and I'd meet him in the lunchroom. But I didn't really have to talk to the teacher. That was a lie. After Darren left, I made sure no one was looking, and I snuck over to Betsy's cubby, where she was busy unstuffing her coat.

"Hi," I said.

She didn't say anything, which was pretty normal, but usually she *looked* at me while she didn't say anything, and this time she wasn't looking at me, so that didn't seem normal at all. I didn't like it.

"Hey, um, Betsy, do you know how to play Pokémon?" I asked her.

Betsy did look up at me then, and she looked confused-mad. Which was not a look that made me happy. I did my best to try to explain to her.

"Because all the cool kids play Pokémon," I said, "and I'm cool now, so I'm learning it, and I thought if you knew too, then you could be cool with me and then we could still sit next to each other at lunch. Wouldn't that be good?" I thought it sounded good. "Anyway, if you don't know Pokémon, I could teach it to you. When I get better, I mean. I'm still not very good."

I must not've been doing a very good job explaining about Pokémon and being cool and lunch and everything, because Betsy went from looking confused-mad to just mad-mad. Which was even worse.

But I didn't get a chance to explain any better, because Betsy started talking then, and even though it took her a long time to get the words out—longer than normal—I waited for her to say what she wanted and didn't interrupt because Betsy hated when you interrupted her before she was done, and I was nice. And cool.

"N-n-n-n-*no*." That's what she told me. "Y-y-you are n-*not* c-c-cool."

I couldn't believe I waited for *that*.

Then she stormed off to the lunchroom. She forgot her lunch bag in her cubby, and I thought about bringing it to her, but then I decided not to. I wasn't feeling very nice right then.

Just cool.

That afternoon was the first lunch of the whole school year where I didn't get any gummy bears.

still.

"W hat the heck is your sister doing in there anyway?"
I asked Erlan when I was over at his apartment. We
were playing Operation, only we couldn't play it in the quilt
fort because Erlan's sister Ainyr was in there crying.

"She broke up with her boyfriend or something," Erlan
told me. "She won't shut up about it either."

That made me so surprised I dropped the funny bone I
was tweezering out and the game buzzed at me. "She has a
boyfriend?" I asked. "She's only in seventh grade."

Erlan took the tweezers. "She's in eighth," he said. He

got the funny bone easy. "And she doesn't have a boyfriend anymore. That's what she's so upset about."

"Oh."

"Anyway, she's being a real baby. They only went out for like a week." He said that loud enough for Ainyr to hear from inside the fort.

"You shut up, Erlan!" she shouted at him.

Erlan handed me the tweezers, and I looked for the best bone to remove. The Adam's apple or the charley horse or the butterflies in the stomach. "I don't think I'll ever go out with anyone," I told Erlan. "It sounds awful."

He rolled his eyes. "You don't even know. Yesterday Ainyr spent two hours deleting all the photos of him off her phone. Two hours! You know how many photos that is? They only went out a week!"

"I'm gonna punch you, Erlan!" Ainyr screamed.

"No you won't!" Erlan shouted back. "Because you'd have to come out here to do it, and then I'd get my fort back!"

Ainyr didn't leave the fort the whole time I was there. Erlan and I played four games of Operation, and she just cried the whole time.

"Do you still have pictures of Gus on your phone?" I asked Calista the next day after school.

She seemed surprised when I asked her that. But sort of happy too. "Sure!" she said. She pulled her phone out of her pocket. "You want to see them?" She started to thumb through to the photos.

I shook my head. "No, thanks," I said. "Can we go visit Hugo and get my donut now?"

Calista frowned, but she put her phone back in her pocket. "Yeah, okay," she told me.

That's how I figured out that Calista still had a boyfriend.

tetherball.

Now that I was cool, I ate lunch with Darren and the other cool kids and played tetherball with them too. I was all right at tetherball, even if I did flinch once when I thought the ball was going to whack me in the head, and Candace Sims laughed at me. At lunchtime, all us cool kids would eat our lunches super-duper fast so we could go outside to meet Sage Moore at the tetherball courts. Sage was Darren's best friend, but he couldn't eat at our same table because he had to eat at the "egg-free" one with the allergy kids.

I didn't mind not having to eat with Sage Moore so much.

"Do you like Carrot Squash?" Sage asked me on Friday when the two of us were next to each other in line waiting for our turn to play tetherball. The way he asked me about it, I felt like I was taking a test. Like there was only one right answer to the question, and he already knew I was going to get it wrong.

"I don't know," I said slowly. I didn't want to get the answer wrong, but I didn't want to lie either. "I've never had it."

Sage laughed so hard when I said that that he started to choke on his own spit. "Oh, my God!" he said between chokes. "You've never *had* it!"

Candace reached around me in line and pounded on Sage's back. To stop the choking, I guess. I hadn't even thought to do that, to pound on Sage's back to help him stop choking.

Then again, I didn't really care if Sage Moore choked so much. (That was not a very nice thing to think, maybe.)

(But it was true.)

"Carrot Squash isn't a food," Darren told me. Darren was so good at tetherball that he could play and talk at the same time. "It's a video game," he said, and he whacked the ball. *Whack!* Nasim Johnson whacked it back. *Whack!* "It's really cool." *Whack!* "You'd like it." *Whack!* "You're a rabbit"—*whack!*—"and you go around killing talking carrots"—

whack!—"that commit crimes." *Whack!* "When they die, all their carrot juice splatters everywhere." The rope wrapped around the pole too high for Nasim to get it, and Darren beat her. She went to the end of the line. Lizzy was next.

"Oh," I said. I was sort of embarrassed that I thought that Carrot Squash was a food. But then I figured if the video game people didn't want everyone to think it was a food, then they shouldn't have named it something that *sounded* like a food. So really it was their fault. "Is it rated E?" I asked.

Sage started choking again, and Candace reached around me to pound his back some more. I was pretty sure she rolled her eyes at me when she did it, but I decided not to notice.

"No," Darren told me. He only had to whack the ball once and it spun spun spun around the pole until it got so high Lizzy couldn't reach it even when she jumped up on her tippy-toes. "It's Teen."

"Oh," I said, when Candace stepped up to play. I put my hands in my pockets. "Then I can't play it. I'm only allowed to play games that are rated E."

Sage was still choking.

"Do you want my juice?" I asked him, since Candace was playing tetherball now and couldn't pound his back anymore. I still had a little juice left over from lunch. "I can go get it from my lunch sack."

Sage looked at me like I was crazy, but I knew I wasn't.

"To help with the choking," I explained. But he just shook his head. Which was fine with me, because it was probably a bad idea to share juice with someone who kept choking anyway.

Betsy stopped eating lunch in the cafeteria. Four straight days, and she wasn't there. She never came out to the blacktop either. Once I remembered to watch her when we were on our way to the lunchroom, so I could figure out where she went, and I found out it was the library. She went to the library every day.

Why would someone go to the library during lunch? You're not allowed to eat in the library. Didn't Betsy get hungry?

I wondered what she did with all those gummy bears if she wasn't allowed to eat them.

helpful hints.

I still wanted to be friends with Betsy, even if that was hard now. Because of me being cool and her not. I decided the best thing I could do was to do a lot of noticing about exactly what the cool kids did, and then tell Betsy to do those things so she could learn how to be cool too.

Helpful hints, that was what she needed.

It was going to be really helpful, actually, because by the end, Betsy would know all the rules for being cool—the ones the cool kids never told you themselves—and who wouldn't want to know that?

The only problem was that Betsy didn't seem to want to talk to me too much anymore. Probably because she was so embarrassed about not being cool. Which made it hard for me to tell her all my helpful hints. But I finally figured out a way to do it. I left a note in Betsy's desk every morning before school started. A new helpful hint every day.

Don't ever be last in the line to go to lunch.

That was one of my helpful hints. I noticed that was one of the things about being cool, that you always had to get to the lunchroom near the front of the class.

Sing fake words to the songs during chorus.

That was another helpful hint. I noticed that one too. Whenever Mrs. Chilcoat came in to do chorus with us, all the cool kids stood in the back and didn't sing the real words we were supposed to. Some of them were just quiet, no noise at all. But some of the coolest kids, like Sage, made up their own words. Like when Mrs. Chilcoat was teaching us the song "Waltzing Matilda," Sage kept singing "farting fat Hilda" instead. Which, as far as I could tell, didn't make any sense, but it must've been pretty funny because all the cool kids in the back near us were laughing so hard with their hands over their mouths that they almost got in trouble. So I figured that was a pretty cool thing to do.

All my notes to Betsy were really helpful hints, I thought. And I left them right where Betsy would be sure to find them, at the very front of her desk, every morning. And I knew Betsy could read them. Betsy was a really good reader.

Only, for some reason, Betsy never did any of the things that the helpful hints said to do. She kept leaving for lunch at the back of the line, way behind me and all the other cool kids. She kept standing exactly where she always did when Mrs. Chilcoat came in for chorus, and she never sang any fake words.

I kept leaving the helpful hints, though. A new one in Betsy's desk every morning. Because if Betsy didn't figure out how to be cool, then we couldn't hang out anymore. And I sure did miss hanging out with Betsy.

second best.

"You should run for vice president of the class, Albie," Darren told me while we were in line for tetherball. It was Candace and Sage playing. Candace was winning.

"Really?" I said. My stomach was grumbling from only eating my bagel at lunch, not my kimchi. The week before, Nasim said kimchi smelled, and even though Darren told her to shut up, I didn't want to eat something that smelled anymore. "How come?"

"Duh, 'cause it's only the second-best job you can have in the class," Darren said.

"What's the best one?" I asked.

"President, dummy." Darren still called me "dummy" sometimes, even though he was my friend now, only he said it while he was laughing and not laughing *at* me I didn't think, so I figured maybe it was okay. Even if I didn't actually like it a whole lot.

"What does vice president get to do again?" Lizzy asked. Lizzy and Nasim were making bead bracelets while they waited for tetherball. "Is that the calendar one?"

"No, secretary makes the birthday calendar," Sage told her. He jumped up to hit the tetherball but missed and Candace got it instead. *Whack!* "Vice president switches off the computers at the end of class and makes sure all the lights are turned off when we leave the room. Treasurer takes the hot lunch count to the office, and safety officer carries the first aid kit in fire drills."

"The president is the one who takes attendance," Darren said, stepping up next to play tetherball after Candace whacked Sage out. "That's the one I'm going to be."

That made me confused. "How do you know you're going to be president if nobody's voted yet?"

"*Duh,*" Darren said as he held up the ball to serve, and Sage snorted as he passed me to go to the back of the line. "Who else do you think would win it?"

"I don't know," I said. "I think Aleef would be pretty good at taking attendance, or Grace, or—" I stopped talking because I realized no one was playing tetherball. Instead,

Darren and Sage and Candace and Nasim and Lizzy were all looking at me funny. That's when I realized that Darren hadn't really been asking me a question. "You'd be a good president," I said to Darren. That seemed like the right thing to say.

Darren nodded when I said that, so I knew it was right. He held the tetherball up again to serve. "Thanks. And you'd be an awesome VP." I smiled at that. "I'll make sure no one else runs so you'll win for sure. Then we can be in charge together." And that time he whacked the tetherball good and hard.

That made me feel good, and while I waited in line for my turn at tetherball, I started to wonder why I'd been thinking before that turning off the lights was a stupid job. It was going to be a great job. I was going to be *awesome* at it.

a note
in my desk.

Stop leaving dumb notes in my desk. I don't want to talk to you.

That was what the note said that I found in my desk Friday morning.

I didn't know who the note was from, or why anybody would think it was *me* leaving dumb notes in their desk. I only left things in Betsy's desk, and those were super-helpful hints to help her be cool like me.

I wanted to leave my helpful hint in Betsy's desk that morning too: *Wear the low kind of socks, not the high ones.* But Betsy was already sitting at her desk early, so I couldn't. I put it in her cubby instead.

meet the kasteevs.

We went over to Erlan's apartment to watch the very first episode of their television show on Friday night, me and Mom and Dad. A pilot, that's what the TV show was called, like it was going to fly an airplane or something.

Television is weird.

Erlan's brothers and sisters all had friends over too, and there were a couple extra adults, so there wasn't much room. Erlan's parents brought out folding chairs, but there still weren't enough for everybody, so a bunch of us kids ended up sitting on the floor. We had popcorn and soda, which normally I wasn't allowed to drink after dinnertime, but Mom said it was okay just this once. The grown-ups ate veggie sticks.

"Aren't you excited?" I asked Erlan. "You're going to be on TV!"

He shrugged. He didn't seem too excited.

Anyway, *I* was excited.

When the show came on, everyone shushed to watch it. At the very beginning, after the title *Meet the Kasteevs,* they showed Erlan's parents, really big on the screen, then all the kids, one by one.

"Alma!" a voice on the screen said. And then there was a shot of Erlan's big sister Alma cuddling a kitten. It wasn't the Kasteevs' kitten, so I didn't know where it came from, but when I tried to ask, I got shushed.

"Ainyr!" the voice said. There was Ainyr, putting on lipstick in her mirror. I didn't even know she wore lipstick.

Then there was "Roza!" and "Erik!" and "Karim!" and they all did things too, so you could get to know which kid was which, I guess. "Erlan!" was last, and what he did when he was on-screen was give the Vulcan salute. "Hey!" I said, and laughed, because that made me happy.

When that happened, I looked next to me, and I could tell that even Erlan was smiling. Just a little bit.

It was a good show. It turned out the first episode was Erlan and his brothers' birthday party, so that was fun to watch because I'd been there in real life. They even showed me on camera once, when we were playing musical plates, except my face was blurred out, so you couldn't tell it was me if you didn't know. *"No release!"* Erlan and I both screamed at once, and giggled.

We got shushed again, but it was worth it.

After the show, Erlan came over to my apartment for a sleepover. "You can have the good sleeping bag if you want," I told him while we were setting up in the living room. "Since you're a big famous TV star."

Erlan threw a pillow at my head. "Shut up," he said. "Just treat me normal, okay? You always have to treat me normal."

I thought about that. And then I picked up the pillow, and I whacked him with it. "Like that?" I said, laughing.

Erlan laughed too. He picked up my pillow. "Exactly," he said, and he whacked me back.

We had a very normal pillow fight.

I guess it wasn't too bad, having a big famous TV star for a best friend.

donut cereal.

Calista didn't usually come over on the weekends, only sometimes. She didn't usually come over in the mornings either, but Dad had a big project coming up and Mom had moved her Pilates schedule, so they said that might happen more. I didn't mind.

"Can we get donuts?" I asked Calista first thing, as soon as Mom closed the door behind her. I was still in my pajamas, but I would change for donuts. I would do almost anything for donuts.

Calista scrunched up her face, thinking. I didn't know

exactly what was going on in her brain, because that was a thing you could never know 100 percent for sure, but if I had to guess, I'd bet that she was thinking about whether she should let me go get donuts, which were delicious, or if she should make me have a healthy breakfast, which was *not* delicious.

I guess the healthy part won, because she pulled the box of Cheerios out of the cupboard.

"Aw, *man*," I said.

"What?" Calista said, unlatching the dishwasher to find a clean bowl. "I thought you said you wanted donuts. So"— she popped the lid on the box and poured out a bowlful— "donut cereal."

I inched my way over to the counter. I knew Calista was being silly, because for one thing I knew the difference between real donuts and Cheerios, and donuts tasted way better. Also, I could tell a trick to force me to eat a healthy breakfast when I saw one. But if I *had* to eat a healthy breakfast, maybe thinking it was a bowlful of mini donuts wasn't the worst thing in the world.

"Thanks," I told Calista, and I grabbed my bowl of mini-donut cereal and went to the fridge to get the milk.

While I ate breakfast and Calista sipped her coffee from downstairs, we worked on our superheroes, and I was extra careful not to drip any milk drops on mine. Calista said Donut Man was getting really good, and that time, I could tell she wasn't being silly.

"You really do love donuts, don't you, Albie?" she asked me while I slurped up the last of my milk on my spoon.

"Yep," I said, because that was the truth.

Calista smiled at that. "I think I just figured out what to get you for your birthday," she said.

I sat up straight in my chair. "You did?"

She nodded.

"Is it a donut?"

"Not telling."

"I bet it's a donut."

Calista laughed. "You'll just have to wait and see, won't you?"

I pushed my bowl to the middle of the table and pulled out a fresh piece of paper. "It's a donut," I said again. And I started on another drawing of Donut Man, with his arms reaching high up into the sky. He was going to be holding the world's biggest donut, I decided. It was going to be my best drawing yet.

nobody.

On Monday morning I got to school early, so I went to the drinking fountain to play Pokémon, but right when I got there, everyone got up and left.

I thought that was weird.

"Hi, Darren!" I said to Darren as he walked away. But he kept walking, didn't even turn around.

That was kind of weird too.

During first recess, I couldn't find Darren at all. He wasn't playing tetherball like he normally was. Nobody else was there either.

That was weirder.

Then at lunch when I went to sit down at the table, Darren put his hand on the bench, right where I was about to sit, and said, "What do you think you're doing, dummy?" And he didn't say "dummy" the way he did before, where it was mean-but-not-really. He said "dummy" the way he had before *that,* where it was actually mean.

"I'm, um . . ." I glanced around. Nobody would look at me. "I was going to eat lunch?" I wondered why he was asking. That's what everybody did at lunchtime—eat lunch.

"Not here you're not," Darren told me. "We don't want liars here."

"Oh," I said. "Okay." Even though I was sort of confused about what he was talking about. Because I was pretty sure he meant me. And I was not a liar.

"Why did you tell everyone that kid Erlan was your best friend?" Candace said, slapping her panda lunch box on the table. "Just so people would think you were cool?"

"Erlan is my best friend," I said. I was just standing, because even though Darren had moved his hand, I didn't think I was allowed to sit down yet. I didn't know what to do. I was confused about the rules again. "We've been best friends since we were four. He lives down the hall."

"Liar," Candace said. She flipped the tabs on her lunch box. "I watched the show on Friday, and you weren't in it."

"I *was,*" I said.

"No you weren't," Lizzy said. "Candace told us. They

had a birthday party with *all their friends,* and you weren't there. You're such a liar. Go sit over there."

I looked at Darren. "But . . . ," I said. Darren was my friend. He said I was cool.

"Go sit over there, *dummy,*" Darren said. He didn't even look up at me.

I ate lunch at the far end of the table, with nobody even near me. They were all scooched over tight on the other side, like I might give them some disease or something.

I was a nobody all day.

I was a nobody the next day too.

And the day after that.

I wished Betsy was there. I guessed I wasn't cool anymore, just like her.

I wished I'd never been cool at all.

not funny.

"What did the calculator say to the student?"

That was Mr. Clifton's joke during math club.

But when he peered at us over his glasses and cleared his throat and said, "You can count on me!" I didn't laugh.

I didn't laugh harder than Savannah, even.

I just sat at my desk with my arms crossed over my chest, grumpy, and said, "You don't count on a calculator. You *add*."

I didn't even raise my hand to say it either.

Behind me, Jacob whispered, "*Whoa.*"

The past couple days, Mr. Clifton's jokes haven't been very funny.

words.

Wednesday at school, Darren Ackleman got in trouble for saying "retard."

"We don't call anyone retarded," Mrs. Chilcoat, the chorus teacher, said, while I did my best to shrink into my chair. "*Retard* is a bad word." She told Darren and everybody that they weren't allowed to use it. Principal Jim even talked about it the next day on the morning announcements, so I guess Mrs. Chilcoat told him about it too.

"From here on out," Principal Jim's voice boomed from the intercom, "the word *retard* is outlawed at P.S. 183." Everyone in Mrs. Rouse's class stared at me the whole time, and I wished there was a secret trapdoor in my seat that would open up, and down below there'd be a lion who would swallow me in one gulp.

But Darren Ackleman doesn't call me "retard" anymore.

Moron.

That's what he called me on Thursday.

Moron. Numbskull. Bozo. Idiot.

Stupid little rat.

Marblehead. Freak. Dum-dum. Hopeless. Lamebrain. Crybaby. F-minus.

Dummy.

That's what he called me on Friday, and every day since.

Dummy.

Dummy.

Dummy.

Darren Ackleman doesn't call me "retard" anymore.

But I think maybe it's not words that need to be outlawed.

no more
helping.

I stopped leaving helpful hints in Betsy's desk. Not because I didn't want to hang out with her anymore. I did. Almost more than anything else. I still missed hanging out with Betsy. A whole lot.

I stopped leaving helpful hints because I decided I didn't want to make Betsy cool anymore. I liked Betsy the way she was, and if she was cool, I didn't think I'd like her as much.

So I stopped leaving helpful hints.

But I kept hoping that one of these days Betsy would

figure out that she liked me again. Because I was pretty sure that she wasn't just embarrassed anymore. I was pretty sure she was mad. And if I could have turned into a whole different person to make her like me again, I would've. But I couldn't. I was just me.

So all I could do was hope.

the worst thing ever.

The worst thing that happens is always the one thing you thought would never, ever happen.

"We're moving," Erlan told me on Saturday. "We're getting a bigger apartment. On the Upper West Side."

After he said that, I felt like I got whacked in the chest with a rock. Hard. I couldn't talk. Not for a whole minute.

"Moving?" I said at last. "That's all the way across the park!"

Erlan nodded, staring down at his macaroni and cheese that was only for the weekends. "Yeah," he said. "But my parents said you can still visit."

I nodded too. "Okay," I told him, because what was I supposed to say? There was nothing good to say when the worst thing ever happens.

Dad said Erlan's family was probably moving because their show got picked up for a full second season. When I asked what that meant, Mom said, "The TV show, Albie. It got very good ratings."

"Oh," I said. "Good for them, I guess." But I didn't mean it.

I was pretty sure I finally figured out what was so bad about having a famous TV star for a best friend.

one vote.

I didn't win vice president. Candace decided she was going to run too, so she won it. I peeked when we were raising our hands for voting, and I only got one vote, and that was from me. No one else voted for me. Not even Betsy.

thoughts.

Calista was always drawing in her sketchbook, but she wouldn't let anybody see. She'd show me the pictures she drew with me at the table when we were making superheroes, but not the ones from her sketchbook. When I asked if I could see just one drawing, she said, "Albie, sometimes people need their own private space to think." Like that was that. But I didn't see how you could think inside a sketchbook.

I took a peek one time, when Calista was in the bathroom. I knew I probably shouldn't, but I just wanted to.

There weren't any thoughts in there. It was all drawings, like I figured, mostly of people. I flipped through and saw people on the subway, people in coffee shops, even people I recognized from going to the park. They were really good drawings.

Then I saw one of a boy that made me stop flipping. I smoothed my hand across the page. He had his hair cut short, cropped above his ears, and the drawing was in pencil so you couldn't tell what color his eyes were, but they were dark, and wide, and sad. You could tell he was sad, even though he was just a drawing, not a real boy you could talk to. The boy was looking off, far away, looking like there was something he wanted, real bad. I wondered what it was. I wished I could get it for him so he'd stop looking so sad.

Then I noticed the tiny speck, a mole, right above the boy's left eyebrow, which is exactly where I have a mole— right above my left eyebrow.

I snapped the sketchbook shut and put it back in Calista's purse before she came out of the bathroom. All afternoon, I wanted to ask her why she'd draw a picture of a boy with a mole just like mine, being sad.

But I didn't. And I didn't look in her sketchbook anymore either. I figured maybe she was right. Sometimes people should be left alone to think their private thoughts.

vulcan salute.

A new family moved into Erlan's apartment. Now when I looked through my kitchen window, I didn't see Erlan in his bedroom. I saw some baby.

I bet it would take that baby at least two years to learn the Vulcan salute.

birthday
cupcakes.

I told Mom I didn't want her to get me any cupcakes for my birthday, that I didn't need any cupcakes, that I didn't like cupcakes as much as donuts, that my birthday wasn't till Saturday anyway, that I didn't even *feel* like celebrating my birthday at school. But she just said, "Nonsense, Albie. Everybody likes celebrating birthdays." And then she took me early to the cupcake place on Lexington and got me two dozen mini cupcakes in a big white box, enough for everyone in my class. There were all different sorts—chocolate with chocolate frosting, chocolate with vanilla frosting, red velvet, Oreo flavor, peanut butter, sprinkles, caramel. Everything. Mom hailed a cab to get to school instead of walking like we normally did so none of the cupcakes would get smooshed. Sitting there in the back of the cab with that big white box on my lap, those cupcakes sure did smell good. The sugar and chocolate and caramel scents were all floating out of the box, landing in my nose, and even though I'd eaten breakfast, my stomach gurgled. I started to get just the littlest bit excited about my birthday. I couldn't wait to eat those cupcakes. I couldn't wait to see everyone's face in my class when they saw how good they looked.

"Have a wonderful day, Albie," Mom told me when the cab stopped outside my school. "I love you."

"I love you too," I told her. She gave me a kiss on the cheek.

Maybe it was going to be a good day-before-my-birthday after all.

That's what I thought.

But when I walked into Mrs. Rouse's class and sat down at my desk with my huge white box, the first thing that happened was that Sage poked me in my side. *Hard.*

"What is that?" he asked me.

I turned around in my chair to look at him. But I was careful not to knock over the cupcakes.

"They're cupcakes," I told him. "For my birthday tomorrow." I smiled at him. Sometimes Sage could seem mean, but I figured he had to be nice to me if he knew it was almost my birthday.

Sage did not seem to be happy that it was almost my birthday. And he didn't do anything nice either. What he did was start screaming, "Mrs. Rouse! Mrs. Rouse!" and running toward the front of the room. Which I thought was weird.

There was a poke in my other side. I turned around in my seat that way.

It was Darren. He didn't seem happy about my almost-birthday either. "Don't you know that cupcakes have *eggs* in them?" he asked me.

"What?" I asked. Because I thought that was a weird question. And I was confused.

Sage was still shouting, "Mrs. *Rouse*! Albie brought *cupcakes* into the classroom!"

I looked back at Darren. "What's wrong with cupcakes?" I asked.

Darren rolled his eyes at me. "Sage is allergic to eggs, dummy. That's why there's a sign on the door." He pointed to the door and the sign with the crossed-out egg. "It's been there all year." I *knew* it had been there all year. Darren didn't have to tell me that. He didn't have to call me "dummy" either. That was just mean.

Then it seemed like everyone was up out of their seats, shouting or talking or coming over to see what was going on. Mrs. Rouse was flicking the lights on and off, but it wasn't helping any.

"Why'd you bring eggs in the classroom?" Nicole asked me. "Did you want Sage to get sick?"

"Mrs. Rouse gave all the parents a letter, remember?" Tia said. "You don't remember?"

"Albie, you know you're supposed to leave outside food in the cafeteria."

"Why'd you do that?"

"What's *wrong* with you?"

I wanted to tell them all that I just forgot. That I thought cupcakes were different. That I didn't remember about the food rule, because it was my birthday. That maybe I never knew cupcakes had eggs in them, because I never made a cupcake before. Or maybe I did know that, and I just forgot. But everyone was yelling at me, or talking at me, or asking me questions, and the lights were flickering, and I couldn't think. My brain wasn't working. I sat in my desk with those stupid cupcakes in their stupid white box, with everyone around me staring. I just bit my lip and stayed quiet.

I was not allowed to cry.

Finally the lights flicked enough that everyone stopped talking. Mrs. Rouse told everyone to go back to their seats, and they finally did.

"Simmer down, class," Mrs. Rouse said. "It's okay."

Mrs. Rouse said it wasn't a big deal, Sage would be fine. "Albie, we'll put your cupcakes in the cafeteria, okay? And then you can pick them up to take home after school is out. Would someone like to volunteer to take them, please?"

I should have paid attention when Darren volunteered to take the cupcakes. I should've known. But I was still biting my lip so hard, thinking about eggs and birthdays and allergies and not crying, and I didn't think about it.

I guess that's something I do a lot—not thinking.

After school Mr. Paul, the lunch aide, let me into the cafeteria kitchen to get the cupcakes. He pointed to the fridge, and I opened it and found the white box on a shelf. Someone had written my name on the side in black marker so it would be easy to find. *Albin Schaffhauser, Room 317.*

"You need help with the box?" Mr. Paul asked me.

"No, thanks," I said, and I slid it out of the fridge. The box was cold.

DUMMY

That's what was written on the top of the box, in big scribbly letters, so fat I couldn't miss it.

I bit my lip again and then, after I checked to make sure Mr. Paul wasn't looking, I opened up the box.

The cupcakes were still there. Two dozen, lined up in neat little rows.

And every single one had a fat, smooshed thumbprint, right in the middle.

I slapped the lid back closed and dumped the box into the trash can. The whole thing.

"Hey!" Mr. Paul called after me as I stomped out of the kitchen. "Kid! Don't you want your cupcakes?"

I didn't even bother to answer.

something
you'll really
love.

We had a birthday dinner on Saturday, just me and Mom and Dad, because I said I didn't want a party. I didn't want a party because Erlan couldn't come anyway because of filming stuff, and Betsy was still mad at me, and Calista had that day off, and I hated pretty much everyone else, so who cared. We had Chinese food. Big whoop.

When Mom asked me how everyone at school liked the cupcakes, I said, "They were great." Which was a lie, but so what.

Mom got me a book. Something about a hatchet, whatever that was. "Because you loved *Johnny Tremain* so much," she said.

Dad's present was in a big box. "I think it's something you'll really love," he told me. I got excited when I first pulled back the wrapping paper, because I saw a wing, an airplane wing, on the cover of the box, and I felt my heart leap up in my chest. It was a new model airplane, I knew right away. Another airplane just like my A-10 Thunderbolt, maybe a bomber or one of the gliders, and Dad was going to help me work on that one too and then we could display them both in the living room, and it would be awesome.

It wasn't another airplane.

Well, it was an airplane. But not another one.

"A real live A-10 Thunderbolt!" Dad said, smiling like he thought he got me the greatest present in the whole universe. "Isn't that marvelous? It's just like the plane in the museum you liked so much. Don't you remember, Albie? I thought we could put it together, just you and me. Albie? Where are you going?"

I didn't even say anything. Just slammed my bedroom door.

flying.

It turned out that dumb old A-10 Thunderbolt from the Sea, Air, and Space Museum didn't fly at all. I don't know if it was because I put it together all wrong, or maybe it was never going to fly in the first place, but all I know is that when I cranked open my window and shoved it outside, it slammed right down to the ground eight stories below without even trying to soar. A man on the sidewalk who was walking right nearby looked up and cursed, but he couldn't tell it was me who did it, and anyway I wouldn't've cared if he could. All I could think was how I spent a whole year and a half working on that stupid airplane, all by my-self, and now it was smashed to bits on the sidewalk. Pieces everywhere.

Good.

I hoped Dad would say, "Hey, Albie, I just remembered I *already* bought you an A-10 Thunderbolt a year and a half ago. Where is it? I'm ready to help you finish it now." Then I could say, "I threw it out the window. It's nothing but smithereens now." And then I could see the look on his face.

But Dad would never ask. I knew he'd never ask.

I decided I didn't like birthdays anymore.

changing channels.

When I woke up the next morning and opened the door, that new A-10 Thunderbolt from Dad was sitting right outside my bedroom in its box, with the bow still on top.

I thought about throwing it out the window. I really did.

Instead I scooped it off the floor and put the box on the top shelf of my closet and put five towels on top of it so I couldn't see it. Then I closed the closet door.

When I propped up the cardboard TV Calista made against my bedroom doorway and lay flat on my stomach, I could see all the way down the hallway, straight through to where the Living Room Channel was playing.

Dad on his treadmill, that's what was on that channel. Running, running, running. Getting sweaty under the armpits. Not answering the phone when it rang. Not noticing the drippy faucet in the kitchen that would've driven Mom crazy. Not asking what happened to the A-10 Thunderbolt box with the bow on top. Not seeing me, for twenty minutes, lying on the floor of my bedroom, staring at him through a cardboard TV.

I pushed all the buttons on Calista's cardboard remote, but the channel never changed.

sad.

Before I even tugged down the covers on Monday, I knew it would be a day not even donuts could solve. I told Calista that when she came over early to help get me ready for school.

"It'll be all right, Albie, I promise." That's what Calista said. "Get up, okay? We have to leave soon or you'll be late. And I'll be there to pick you up when school gets out, and I have a special birthday present for you, and we can get donuts too if you need them. Three kinds."

I curled tighter into a ball under the covers. "No," I told her.

"Albie . . ." Calista sat down on the foot of my bed. *You're being silly.* That's what I thought she was going to tell me. That's what Mom would've said. *You don't have a choice, so just get out of bed already.* That's what Dad would've told me.

Calista didn't say those things.

Instead, she pulled the covers gently back from my face, and when I felt her do that, I opened my squeezed-shut eyes to look at her, even though she was blurry from the tears I'd been trying not to cry.

"Oh, Albie." That's what she said. "What happened?"

And so I told her. I sat up, and I sniffled, and I wiped at my face, and maybe I even cried a little bit more while I said it all, but right then I didn't even really care that much. I told Calista everything.

I told her about the stupid baby who didn't even know the Vulcan salute.

I told her about how much I missed gummy bears.

I told her about how it stunk to not be a famous TV star, even though I never knew before I wanted to be one in the first place.

I told her about how I hated Darren Ackleman more than a million hissing cockroaches.

I told her about the A-10 Thunderbolt, the first one and the second one, and the smashing and the smithereens.

I told her about the cupcakes.

I told her about "retard" and "freak baby" and "dummy."

I told her that I couldn't go to school. Not again. Not ever.

And when I was done with all the telling, I got back under my covers and curled into a ball, my knees against my stomach, and Calista rubbed my back in tiny circles, and I let her.

"You're right," she told me softly. "This is too big for donuts."

After Calista left me under the covers, I kept waiting and waiting for her to come back and tell me it was time for me to get ready already. But she never did. And after a while, I was pretty sure it was past when we should've been out the door. And after a *long* time, I knew it was past then. But Calista never came to get me. So I just stayed under the covers, curled into a ball, knees to stomach, and I cried.

After a while I ran out of tears, so I pushed back the covers and looked around my bedroom. No Calista. I set my bare feet down on the floor and walked to the door and peered into the hallway. No Calista. I walked down the cold hall into the dining room.

Calista was sitting at the table, reading one of my dad's magazines about money. She jumped up when she saw me. "Oh, good!" she said, and she seemed really happy to see me, not mad that I probably almost definitely was late for school. "You're up!"

"I think I'm late," I told her.

Calista looked at the clock. "Yup," she said. "About forty minutes."

I scratched at my hair, which was still messy from sleeping. "Then I guess we should probably get going so I'm not even later, huh?"

Calista tilted her head to the side, like *she* was the one who was confused. "I thought you said this was bigger than a donut day," she said.

"Well, yeah, but—"

"Everyone deserves a sad day once in a while," Calista told me. "Sometimes things are too big for cheering up. Sometimes the best way to make things better is just to let yourself be sad for a little bit."

I sat down at the table, and Calista pushed a plate of toast at me. She'd already spread jam on it—strawberry, my favorite. I took a small bite.

"Thanks," I told her.

She watched me chew for a while.

"What do people do on sad days?" I asked when I was pretty much done with my toast. "If they can't be cheered up?"

Calista thought about that. "Did you know I've never been to the Bronx Zoo?" she asked me after a while.

I didn't think going to the zoo on such a gray, gray day would be any fun, because for one thing there wouldn't be anybody there. But Calista said that was exactly why it would be fun, because we'd have the zoo all to ourselves. So after I finished all my toast and two glasses of orange juice too, I changed into my warmest clothes plus my puffy jacket, and Calista grabbed two umbrellas, and we headed to the subway.

It was a long ride to the Bronx Zoo. Long and gray and quiet. There was hardly anyone on the train, because it was a drizzly Monday at ten o'clock in the morning, probably. When the subway popped up aboveground, it was even grayer in the Bronx than it had been in Manhattan.

When we finally got to the zoo, the man at the ticket booth looked surprised that anyone was there. The rain was starting to turn into snow, tiny slushy flakes, and I was cold, and I was starting to think that coming to the zoo was probably the worst idea Calista had ever had, and if I were in school right now maybe Darren Ackleman would be calling me names but at least I'd be warm. But Calista paid the ticket man for both our tickets, and when he gave me a funny look, she said, "School in-service day." Whatever that meant.

I'd been to the Bronx Zoo before, about five times probably, so Calista said I could pick where to go first. I picked the Congo exhibit, because that one was my favorite. Calista read her map, and she found the way pretty quick.

There was no one else but us at Congo, so we could watch the gorillas for as long as we wanted, without anybody or their baby pushing in front of us. One mom gorilla smashed her face right up against the window so me and her were face-to-face, and she slobbered all over the glass. Calista said she must've been trying to give me kisses, and that made me laugh.

"This is pretty fun so far, huh, Albie?" Calista said.

I stopped laughing. "I thought you weren't going to try to cheer me up," I told her.

"No, sir," she said. "I wouldn't dream of it. This is your sad day."

"Good," I said. "Because I'm still sad."

After Congo, Calista picked the reptile house, which was warm warm warm—so warm that the glass in front of the snakes and turtles was half steamed up. But that was okay by me. Me and Calista peeled off our coats and shook all the slushy snow out of our umbrellas and got to work being sad.

"Albie, look at this!" Calista shouted all of a sudden while I was watching some tortoises. That was another good thing about going to the zoo on a gray, gray day—no one cared if you shouted. "You have to see this."

I ran over, and I saw it. Probably the grossest, coolest thing I ever saw in my whole life. Behind the glass where Calista was pointing, there was a python, big as a tree and long as one too. And I'd never believe it if I hadn't seen it with my own eyes, but I swear that python was *eating a pig.* The pig was already dead—Calista said the zookeepers probably put him in frozen, like a giant pig pop—and that was a good thing for him, I bet, because he was getting *swallowed.* The python had his jaws stretched wide, way way past his eyeballs, and the pig was already halfway down. All you could see was the pig's back legs sticking out past the python's fangs, plus its pink piggy tail.

"*Whoa,*" I said.

We watched for probably a full hour, till our breath steamed up the glass too much to watch much more and our feet started to get sore. That python was such a slow eater that he still hadn't even finished by the time we left the reptile house.

"Bye, snake," I said as we left. "Bye, pig."

"I think you mean 'bye, *lunch,*'" Calista told me.

For a second that got me laughing so hard I almost forgot it was a sad day.

On the subway ride back home, I told Calista, "That was a good sad day."

She smiled. "I'm glad, Albie." She looked at the zoo map in her hand for a second and then held it out to me. "You want to keep this, as a souvenir?" I took it. And I was looking for the reptile house on the map when Calista told me, "You have to go back to school tomorrow, you know. This was your only sad day."

"I know," I said. Because I did. You couldn't let every day be a sad day.

"It's probably going to be tough," Calista told me, "at school tomorrow. But you'll get through it. You can be brave, right? You're good at that."

I pushed my nose closer to the map. "Caring and thoughtful and good," I said.

"What was that?" Calista asked.

I shook my head.

"Hey, Calista?"

"Yeah?"

"Should I tell Mom and Dad?" I asked her. "About going to the zoo today for my sad day instead of going to school?"

Calista bit her bottom lip for a while before she answered me. "I would never tell you to lie to your parents, Albie," she said at last.

"But if I don't lie," I said, thinking things through, "then they'll probably be mad at you because you didn't make me go to school."

"Probably," Calista agreed.

"And you'll probably get in trouble," I told her.

"I would imagine so, yes," she said.

I looked back at the map. My brain was feeling fuzzy a little bit, like when I tried to figure out Wei's tip for Chinese food. "I don't think I'll tell them," I said.

Calista didn't say anything about that, just stared out the window at the black of the subway tunnel passing by as we rode. I folded up the zoo map and put it in my pocket.

the surprise
in the fridge.

"A lbie, what's this?" Mom asked when she opened up the fridge to start dinner after Calista had gone home.

"I don't know," I said, without even looking. Because how would I know what was in the fridge?

"It's for you," Mom told me. And that made me look up. For me?

I rushed to the fridge, and sure enough, there was a big brown box on one of the shelves. All the lettuce and cheese had been pushed over to the side so it would fit. On the side in bubble letters it said, *Happy Birthday, Albie!*

Calista's handwriting.

"My present!" I told Mom. I couldn't believe I'd forgotten. I'd never forgotten about a birthday present before in my whole life. "Calista said she brought me something."

"Well, let's see what it is." And Mom pulled out the box and set it on the table. I helped her tug back the lid.

It was a giant cake, shaped like a huge, perfect donut. Vanilla, it looked like, rounded on the sides like a real giant donut with a hole in the middle and everything. There was thick chocolate glaze dripping down the sides and sprinkles all over the top.

"Cool!" I said.

"Now, isn't that sweet?" Mom said. I laughed, and she looked at me. "What?"

"It's a donut cake," I told her. "So it *has* to be sweet!"

Mom laughed, too, and hip-bumped me. "Looks like the perfect after-birthday dessert," she said.

The donut cake was so delicious that for a second I forgot it was still a sad day.

rain in
new york.

When it rains in New York, no one knows where to walk. The streets fill with rainwater at the corners of every block, and even though it doesn't look too deep, if you step off the sidewalk in the wrong spot, it'll swallow up your whole sneaker. So when it rains in New York, nobody crosses at the crosswalks. People walk right across the middle of Fifth Avenue in traffic, and the cars honk and the people shout and the rain slurs up all the noise.

When it rains in New York, people rush rush rush with their necks hunched low in their jackets and men stand at every street corner shouting, "Umbrella! Umbrella, five dollars!" The price always starts at five when it's just sprinkling, then goes up to fifteen when it's really pouring. Which, if you ask me, is just too bad, because that's really when you need an umbrella most.

When it rains in New York, rich people's dogs wear miniature raincoats and plastic slippers that pinch their paws, and kids giggle and shriek and splash in the puddles.

When it rains in New York, the playgrounds are empty and the buses are full. People cram together under the awning outside the bagel shop and talk too loudly on their phones.

When it rains in New York, the garbage cans at every corner are stuffed with the twisted bits of broken umbrellas. When it rains in New York, everyone is happy that the building at 59th and Lex is under construction, when just the day before they said the scaffolding made their eyes sore.

And when it rains in New York, people who aren't paying attention, like Darren Ackleman, because they are too busy doing something else, like making fun of someone walking with his not-a-babysitter home from school, get sprayed right in the face by dirty rainwater splashed by a passing bus. Soaked, head to toe.

I like when it rains in New York.

putting
it together.

I didn't mean to take that A-10 Thunderbolt down off the closet shelf. I really didn't. I meant to leave it up there forever.

But somehow, when I wasn't thinking too good maybe, I took it down. And I opened the box. And I peeled the tape off the tops of the little plastic bags. Carefully, so none of the tiny pieces would spill out.

And I started to put it together.

It was easier this time, since I didn't have to go so slow,

waiting for Dad to help. It was easier this time, because I'd done it before. The directions made more sense. The pieces fit together right, exactly perfect.

I didn't mean to build a real model A-10 Thunderbolt. But every day, it got just a little bit bigger.

smart.

Calista and her boyfriend broke up. For real. She didn't tell me at first, but I knew she was sad. Somehow I just knew. And when I asked her about it, she started crying, right there on the couch. Not grown-up crying either, but big, blubbery kid sobs.

"I'm sorry, Albie," she said. Tears were running down her face. "I'm such a mess today. Just ignore me, okay? It's not a big deal. We'll start on your homework."

But when Calista was in the bathroom washing her tears

off, I snuck out of the apartment and down the elevator and outside to the bodega.

"Can I have some ice cream?" I asked Hugo. "I don't have any money, but I'll stack lots of cups tomorrow. Three hundred. A thousand, even."

Hugo tilted his head to the side. "No donuts today?" he asked.

"Calista's sad," I told him.

And when I said that, well, Hugo practically jumped out from behind the counter and leapt to the ice cream fridge. "Here," he said, handing me a pint of mint chip. "Or do you think she'd rather have chocolate? Oh, that sweet girl. Is she okay?"

"I think she'll be all right," I told him. "But she and her boyfriend broke up."

Hugo shook his head. "That boy must be an idiot," he said.

I agreed.

When I left the bodega, I had a plastic bag stuffed full of ice cream—mint chip and chocolate and cherry vanilla and caramel swirl and Heath bar crunch. Hugo said it was on him, I didn't even have to stack cups for it.

Calista practically chewed my head off when I got back inside the apartment. "Where on earth did you *go*?" she yelled at me. She had her phone in her hand. She'd been dialing someone. "You gave me nine heart attacks."

I held out the plastic bag. "It's from Hugo," I told her. I took the ice creams out, one by one, and set them on the table. And then, because I thought she might be worried, I said, "Even though this is ice cream, it isn't an ice cream day. It's a sad day. But I think it's too late to go to the zoo."

"Oh, Albie." And wouldn't you know it, Calista started crying again. But this time it seemed like it was okay. "Come here." And she stretched out her arms and wrapped me in a hug. A tight one.

"You seemed like you needed a sad day," I told her, through the pinch of the hug.

She laughed a tiny laugh. "You were right," she said. She stretched out her arms to look at me. "How did you get so smart?"

I just shrugged.

We ate ice cream sundaes instead of dinner. I didn't ask, but it seemed like, by the time I went to bed, Calista was maybe feeling just the tiniest bit better.

one word.

I was leaving math club when Mr. Clifton stopped me. "Stay for just a second, if you would, Albie. I want to ask you something."

So I stayed.

Mr. Clifton waited until the door had shut behind the last student and then he said, "Is everything okay?" I looked up at him. "You've seemed a little down the last few days."

I frowned.

"Anything you want to talk about?" he asked me.

I shrugged.

I thought Mr. Clifton was going to let me go, but he just

waited, like he thought I'd say something eventually. The bell rang, even, and he still kept waiting.

I guessed I better say *something*.

"This one kid," I told him, "keeps calling me names. 'Dummy.' Stuff like that."

That wasn't the only thing I was sad about, but it was one of the things. I figured it would be a good thing for Mr. Clifton. Teachers always liked to help with that sort of stuff.

Mr. Clifton nodded for a while before he said anything. "Let me ask you something, Albie," he said at last. "Would it bother you if this kid called you a three-toed yellow featherbed?"

I didn't mean to laugh, but I did anyway. A little snot came out of my nose, even. *"No,"* I said, wiping my face with my sleeve.

Mr. Clifton reached behind him without looking and handed me a Kleenex. I took it. "And why not?" he asked me. "Why wouldn't that bother you?"

"Because I'm *not* a three-toed . . ."

"A three-toed yellow featherbed," Mr. Clifton finished for me.

"Yeah." I blew my nose. "I'm not one of those."

He nodded, like that made sense. Then he said, "So why does it bother you when someone calls you a dummy?"

I stopped blowing my nose.

"Look," Mr. Clifton said. There were kids at the window in the door, waiting to come in for the next math club, I could see them, but Mr. Clifton held up a hand to tell them to wait. "I'm not going to say that other kids can't be mean sometimes. Sometimes people say things that are just *awful*." I looked down into my Kleenex. "But *you* know who you are, Albie. You know what you're worth. At least I hope you do." I folded the tissue over on itself once, then twice, then three times. "And you get to decide what words are hurtful to you. If you ask me, 'dummy' shouldn't hurt you one bit."

When I couldn't fold the tissue anymore, I unfolded it.

"Does that make sense, Albie?"

I nodded. "Can I go back to class now?" I asked.

On my way back to class, I thought about what Mr. Clifton said. I wasn't sure he was right, that I got to decide what words hurt me. Because some words just *hurt*. But I let myself think about it anyway. Because Mr. Clifton was smart, so what he said was worth thinking about.

Dummy, I thought to myself as I walked down the hall. *Dummy dummy dummy*. I thought about that word. I thought about the way it sounded, the *m* sound and the *d* and the end like in *Albie*.

One little word.

It *did* hurt when I said it in my head, no matter what Mr. Clifton told me. That word *dummy* poked me in the brain, in the stomach, in the chest, every time I heard it.

Dummy.

Dummy.

Dummy.

But about halfway down the hall, a funny thing started to happen.

The more I rolled that word around in my head, the sillier it sounded.

Dummy rhymes with mummy.

I rolled it around some more.

Dummy like a dumbbell.

I rolled it again.

Crash test dummy.

Ventriloquist dummy.

Dummy gummy funny sunny.

By the time I got to Mrs. Rouse's room, I'd rolled that word around so much, I thought I might just have rolled its sharp edges a tiny bit smoother.

getting where you're going.

I barely talked to Calista the whole way home from school that day. And when we got home, I didn't even wait for her to make my snack. I went straight to my room and closed the door. Then I sat on the carpet, right in front of my dresser, and opened the bottom drawer.

Under all of my pairs of swim trunks that were too small for me to wear anymore, that's where it was. The letter. I pulled it out.

"Albie?" Calista was knocking on the door. "Albie, you okay in there? What's wrong?"

I unfolded the letter and pressed out the creases, one, two.

Dear Mr. and Mrs. Schaffhauser,

That part was easy to read. The rest was harder.

I'm writing in regards to the academic progress of your son, Albin Schaffhauser, which, as you both know, has been a matter of much concern for some time now.

"Albie?"

I didn't have a lock on the door. I guess that was how Calista got in.

"What are you reading?" she asked. She sat down on the carpet, right beside me. "What is that?"

I set the letter down in my lap, and I think my eyes must've been blurry from reading too hard or tears or something, because all I could see was the name of the school in big red letters at the top of the page. MOUNTFORD PREPARATORY SCHOOL. I couldn't read any of the other words.

Not like I'd understand them anyway.

"It's from my old school," I told Calista.

She must've guessed I was upset, maybe by the way I was talking, quiet like a snowflake, because she started rubbing my back in slow little circles. And she didn't say anything, just nodded.

"It's the letter they sent right before my parents decided I should go to a new school. Only I think maybe they didn't really get to decide that."

Kicked out. I'd been kicked out. I couldn't understand all the words on the page, but I knew enough to know that much. I wasn't smart enough, so they kicked me out.

I wasn't even smart enough to read the letter about kicking me out.

"Oh, Albie," Calista said. Her voice was quiet like a snowflake too.

"It's okay," I told her, because she sounded so upset. But it wasn't okay, not really, and I think she knew that too.

We were quiet a long time. We just sat there, me staring at the fuzzy red letters of the school, and Calista rubbing my back in tiny circles.

Calista was the one who spoke first.

"If you could go back to that school," Calista asked me, "right now, would you?"

I thought about it, long and careful. There were things I liked about Mountford. Erlan was there, and I missed seeing him in class and having lunch with him. I missed having lunch with anyone.

But my teachers were nicer now. And math made more sense at this school, because I had Mr. Clifton and math club. And I got to read books I liked, like *Captain Underpants*, and Mrs. Rouse didn't care so much.

And P.S. 183 never sent home a letter about me, saying I wasn't smart enough to go there.

"No," I said. "I guess not."

"So maybe," Calista said slowly, "your old school being a bunch of mean jerks was the nicest thing they could have done for you?" She said it like a question.

I laughed at that, because it was funny, thinking about my old school being a bunch of mean jerks. They sort of *were* a bunch of mean jerks. I wiped at my nose. "Yeah," I said. "Maybe."

And then I thought of something Mr. Clifton had said.

"You can't get where you're going without being where you've been."

Calista raised an eyebrow at me when I said that. "Where did you get a saying like that from?" she asked.

"Mr. Clifton's grandma."

"I like it," Calista told me.

"Me too."

That night when I went to sleep, nothing really had changed. I still wasn't cool. I still didn't have a finished A-10 Thunderbolt in a display case in the living room, or a dad who would help me build one. I still didn't have anyone to sit with at lunch. I still had never got more than seven words right on a spelling test. But things *felt* a little different. Just a tiny titch of a bit.

That's because me and Calista had made a frame out of cardboard, she'd helped me paint it and everything, so it looked just like a fancy one on a museum wall. But hanging inside it wasn't a piece of art. Hanging inside it, high on the back of my bedroom door where no one could see it but me when I was tucked in bed with the door closed ready for sleep, was my letter from Mountford.

I looked at the letter from across the room, squeezing Norm the Bear close to my chest, and I noticed that the red letters at the top of the page went from fuzzy to clear to clearer.

what i could have said.

When my dad walked into my room when I wasn't expecting and saw me working on the A-10 Thunderbolt, almost completed except for the stickers I never got to putting on the first one so they were a little tricky, he seemed really impressed.

"Albie!" he said. He squatted down right there on the carpet to look at the airplane close up. "How did you do this so quickly?"

What I could have said was "I don't know. I'm just good at putting airplanes together, I guess."

What I could have said was "Why? Do you think it looks cool?"

What I could have said was nothing, just a shrug.

I could have said any of those things.

But I didn't feel like it. I felt like telling the truth.

What I said was, "I already put one together before, so this one was easy. I already put together the one that we bought when we went to the Sea, Air, and Space Museum a year and a half ago that you said you'd help me with, but then you forgot. And then when you got me this one for my birthday, I threw that one out the window. And I was going to throw this one out the window too, but I didn't. I put it together instead." And then I looked up at him, and I shrugged, and I said, "Why? Do you think it looks cool?"

I think my dad did not know what to say to that.

I think my dad planned on squatting there forever, with his mouth hanging open, not saying anything.

I went back to putting on the stickers. It took a little bit to figure out which way they should go, but I looked at the instructions for a long time, and eventually I figured it out.

"I'm so sorry, Albie." That's what my dad said after a long time of not saying anything. I'd sort of forgotten he was there. I looked up. "I'm really sorry," he said again.

I just shrugged.

Dad watched me work on the stickers even longer, and I guess his legs must've got tired of squatting, because after a while he scooched down on his stomach, his elbows on

227

the carpet. And he picked up one of the sheets of stickers I hadn't gotten to yet and peeled one off and said, "Where does this one go, do you think?" And we looked at the directions together.

I put most of the A-10 Thunderbolt together by myself. But my dad did help, at the end.

one last hint.

Betsy didn't really need any more helpful hints. She was smarter than me, for sure. But I decided to leave one last one anyway. Even smart people probably like to get a hint every once in a while.

I think you're pretty great how you are.

That's what it said.
It was the truth too.

a note from home.

"Albie?" Mrs. Rouse said on Wednesday. "Do you have a note from home about your absence last week? You never gave me one."

I rubbed the back of my neck where Darren had flicked it on the way back from the pencil sharpener.

"Huh?" I said, still rubbing.

"A note," Mrs. Rouse said again. "About your absence. I need a note from one of your parents letting me know why you were out."

My mouth felt dry all of a sudden. I forgot about my neck. "I . . ." But I closed my mouth, because I wasn't sure what I was going to say.

"Just bring it tomorrow, okay?" Mrs. Rouse told me.

I nodded. Because what else was I supposed to do?

hannah schaffhauser.

That afternoon, while Calista was in the bathroom, I told her I wanted to watch kung fu videos on Mom's laptop, but I didn't. What I did was I found the file on the desktop from when Mom wrote my sick notes, and I opened it. I only had to change a few words.

> Dear Mrs. Rouse,
> Albin was out sick last week. Please excuse his absence.
>
> Sincerely,

And then under the *Sincerely,* Mom always signed her name, Hannah Schaffhauser. In pen.

Printing it wasn't the hard part.

Hannah Schaffhauser

I practiced Mom's signature over and over, down the sides of a piece of scrap paper and up again.

Hannah Schaffhauser

I'd found an old letter she'd signed in her desk, and I was trying to copy all the letters just right. That's what I was doing instead of sleeping.

Hannah Schaffhauser

I practiced the way the capital *H* crossed back over itself. I practiced the dip in the big *S.* I practiced the way Mom did the double-*f,* which was super different from the way I did it when I signed my own name.

I practiced and practiced and practiced.

Hannah Schaffhauser

It was a long signature, and hard to get just right.

I couldn't get it perfect, no matter how hard I tried. Only almost perfect.

Hannah Schaffhauser

But almost was better than nothing.

I pushed away the piece of scrap paper and looked at the note I'd printed. All ready for me to give to Mrs. Rouse, except for Mom's signature.

If I signed the note and told Mrs. Rouse it was from my mom, then I'd be lying. And if I got caught, I'd get in trouble.

But if I *didn't* sign it and give it to Mrs. Rouse, then Mrs. Rouse would probably call my mom to ask why I was out, and then Mom would know that I didn't go to school, and then *Calista* would get in trouble. And I didn't think Calista should get in trouble, because what she did was a nice thing, giving me a sad day when I needed a sad day. And it did make me feel better, even if Darren Ackleman still called me "dummy" about nine times every day. It made me feel better because I knew that last Monday, while Darren Ackleman was doing social studies worksheets, I'd seen a python eating a pig. And that was worth a million and a half bad names.

I pressed my pen hard into the paper, and I signed it.

worrying.

When I gave the note to Mrs. Rouse the next morning, all that happened was she read it, and she looked at me, and then she looked back at the note, and she said, "Thank you, Albie. You can sit down now."

That was it.

I don't know what I was so worried about. I didn't get in trouble at all.

the worst worst thing.

The worst thing that happens is always the one thing you thought would never, ever happen.

"Where's Calista?" I asked when my mom picked me up on the blacktop after school that day. Mom never picked me up. It was always Calista.

"Albie," Mom said. She reached her hand out to take my backpack from me, but I didn't want to give it to her. I didn't like the way she said "Albie." It was the way to say it that had bad news after it. "I need to talk to you about something."

"Where's Calista?" I said. We followed the other kids and their nannies and parents out to the sidewalk, and Mom still didn't answer. "Where's Calista?" I asked again, because I thought maybe she didn't hear me. "Is she sick?"

"Albie."

We were on the corner, next to a garbage can overflowing with garbage, and Mom knelt down to look at me while we waited for the light. She looked like she didn't want to say what she was about to say. I felt hot all of a sudden inside my puffy jacket, like I was coming down with a fever.

"Calista isn't going to be your babysitter anymore," my mom said.

I couldn't breathe when she said that. I couldn't blink.

"Albie, sweetie. Look at me."

"Did she get hurt?" I asked. "Did she move?" I couldn't believe Calista would just decide not to be my babysitter without even telling me. She taught me how to draw superheroes. She took me for donut days.

She said I was smart.

"Calista . . ." My mom's eyes darted across the street. The cars were stopped at the light, and she wanted to cross, I could tell, but I wasn't moving. I'd forgotten how. "Calista lied, Albie," my mom said, turning back to me. "I don't feel safe having someone take care of you who I can't trust, so I had to let her go."

"She *lied*?" I asked. That didn't sound like Calista. Calista wasn't a liar.

Mom sighed. "Why didn't you tell me she'd taken you to the zoo last week instead of going to school, Albie? I didn't even find out about it until your teacher called me at work this morning to ask about a suspicious note."

My stomach had a rock in it, a real rock, hard and round and heavy.

"Calista didn't write that note!" I shouted. I saw Sage Moore staring at me as he walked by with his older sister, but I didn't care. This was worth yelling about. "I wrote that note. Calista didn't lie about anything. Call her back and tell her you want her to be my babysitter again." I tugged at my mom's purse, trying to find her phone. "You have to." I tugged and tugged.

"Albie, stop it!" Mom said. She straightened up to standing.

"But you *have* to!" I was crying then, and more kids were staring. Laughing too. But I didn't care about them either. I couldn't believe this was all my fault. I couldn't believe my mom fired Calista and it was all because of me, because I signed my mom's name on a stupid piece of paper. I should've signed it better. If I was better at signing, this never would've happened.

"Mom, you *have* to!"

"I'm sorry, Albie."

That was all she said.

voice mail.

After my mom had to race back to work, I found Calista's phone number on the list of emergency contacts on the bulletin board in the kitchen. I knew I probably shouldn't call it.

I called it.

"*This is Calista.*" It was her voice mail. "*I can't answer the phone right now, so please leave a message.*"

I left a message.

"It's Albie," I said. "I was just calling because . . ." I stopped talking. Because actually, I wasn't so sure what I wanted to say. I'd never called Calista's phone before, and it was weird.

I looked at the fruit in the bowl on the counter. I knew I should finish talking and hang up, because any minute Harriet the cleaning lady was going to be done vacuuming in my parents' room and come out to the kitchen and be mad at me for being on the phone, because it wasn't in her job description to watch children, and it wasn't worth the extra cash.

"It was my fault, about the note," I said into the phone. "I'm sorry."

I wanted to say something else, but I couldn't think of anything. That was all there was to say.

I hung up the phone.

mad.

That night at bedtime, Mom knocked on my bedroom door, because it was closed.

"Time for bed, Albie," she said, even though I was already under the covers. Mom sat down on the edge of my bed. I was reading a new Captain Underpants book, and it didn't even have the fake *Johnny Treeface* title on it, but Mom didn't say anything about that. She tucked the covers up around my armpits, even though I was way too old for tucking. She leaned over and kissed my forehead.

"I love you, Albie," she said.

"You do?" I asked. I couldn't help it.

"Yes." She smoothed back my hair. "You are caring and thoughtful and good." She blinked at me, and that's when I started to wonder if maybe she'd been crying earlier.

"I do the best I can," she told me. She said each word real slow. "At being your mother. I don't always know how, but . . . I try."

I thought that was a weird thing to say. Because I never thought before about being a mom as something you had to try at, like math or spelling. Being a mom was just something you *were*.

"I only want you to be safe," she said, still talking slow. "That's all I want for you. Safe and happy."

I wanted to be mad at her. I wanted to be so, so mad.

"I know," I said. I wriggled my arms out from under the covers and set them on top. "But maybe you don't have to worry about me so much all the time."

"Oh, Albie," Mom said, leaning over close for another kiss on my forehead. "Of course I do. I'm your mother."

new kid.

There was a new kid in school. Darissa, that was her name. I knew because even though she had a different teacher, she was in math club, like me.

"Albie," Mr. Clifton said when he was introducing her to the class, "would you like to be Darissa's buddy this week?"

"Buddy?" I said.

"Sure." He showed Darissa to her seat, the one right next to mine. "Make sure she knows where the nurse's office is, maybe hang out with her during recess, that sort of thing."

"Okay," I said. "I guess."

"She's new to the city too, so maybe you can give her some helpful pointers."

I raised my eyebrows at that. I had *loads* of helpful pointers.

Darissa smiled a friendly smile at me as she scooched into her desk.

"Don't worry," Mr. Clifton told her before he walked back to the front of the room. "You're in good hands with Albie."

I smiled back at the new girl. "I'll tell you everything you need to know," I said.

what got into me.

On Science Friday, it was Betsy's turn to bring something in. She brought in a bug she found hiding under a bench in her apartment lobby. It was a "boxelder bug," she said. She'd looked it up. It was big and mostly black with some bright red marks, and awesome gross red eyes. It was still alive, in a big empty pickle jar. Betsy had poked holes in the lid, and she had some twigs in there and grass, for it to eat, I guess.

It was pretty cool. Maybe not as cool as Darren's dad's bug that he brought in, but it was still alive, which was way better. She went through the aisles so we could all look at it, and when she got to Darren and Sage, they tried to pretend like they weren't interested, but you could tell they really were.

She skipped right past my desk. I think it was probably on purpose, since Betsy seemed like she was still mad at me.

When it was time for questions, I kept raising my hand, but Betsy didn't call on me, only Tasha in the front row. Darren kept laughing every time Betsy answered a question, and making fake stuttering noises to Sage. He was sort of quiet so Mrs. Rouse couldn't hear, but I heard it. I think Betsy did too.

I wish she would've called on me when I had my hand up. I wanted to tell her I thought her bug was the coolest one I ever saw.

Then again, maybe it was good she didn't call on me. I don't think Betsy likes things that are cool.

It happened at recess. Darren stole Betsy's bug, right out of her hands. I saw it from where I was sitting, at the bench, showing the new girl Darissa my Captain Underpants book (which was what I normally read during recess, because of not having any friends). Well, first I heard Betsy shouting, and then I saw that Darren had the bug in the pickle jar, and then I figured out that he'd taken it.

"G-g-g-give m-me that!" Betsy shouted.

Darren was holding it high over his head, and Betsy was

reaching for it, but she couldn't get it. Sage and Candace and them were laughing.

"M-m-make me!" Darren said.

Betsy was trying not to cry, I could tell. Her hands were balled up into fists.

I closed my book.

I stood up.

I left my Captain Underpants book on the bench with Darissa, and I went over.

I didn't know what I was going to do—try to make Darren give the bug back, I guess. I didn't know. I wasn't sure why I wanted to help Betsy so bad, because we weren't friends anymore. She wouldn't talk to me. She wouldn't even *look* at me. But Darren was being mean, and that wasn't right. So I closed my book and I stood up and I went over there.

I was too late.

Before I even got there, Darren unscrewed the lid on the pickle jar, and the bug hopped right out. Betsy scrambled to catch it, but it was too fast. It was zoom, zoom, *gone.* Lost in the bushes.

"Oops!" Darren said. But even I could tell it hadn't been an accident.

What was I supposed to do then?

Darren and Sage and Candace and them walked away, laughing, and I picked the jar up off the grass and handed it to Betsy. It still had the twigs and grass in it.

"Here," I said.

Betsy took it, but she didn't look at me.

She left the lid in the grass.

When we got back to class after recess, Darren's desk was on the ground, toppled over. The papers were falling out everywhere, ripped and torn. His pencils were broken in half. Everyone stopped in the doorway and gasped.

"Who did this?" Mrs. Rouse hollered at us. "Who would do such a thing? This is unacceptable."

We filed into the classroom slowly, one at a time, all staring at Darren and his desk. He was seething angry. Everyone was staring at Darren, shouting by his desk. "What the *heck*? What the *heck*?"

I wasn't staring at Darren, though. I looked over at Betsy. Her eyes were on the wall, not on Darren and his desk. She bit her bottom lip, the way she did when she was nervous, and she just blinked. *Blink. Blink.* Over and over.

"Who *did* this?" Mrs. Rouse said again.

"I did."

It was me who said it, even though it was a lie. I didn't topple over anything.

But I knew who did. And I didn't really think that person should get in trouble when they weren't the person who was mean in the first place.

"Albie!" Mrs. Rouse shouted. She seemed shocked. "What got into you?"

I glanced at Betsy. She seemed shocked too. "I, um . . ." I shrugged. "I was just angry, I guess."

Mrs. Rouse made me help Darren clean up his desk, and then she told me she'd let me know when she'd decided on an appropriate punishment for me. Detention, probably, or worse.

I didn't care. If I couldn't help Betsy get her bug back, I figured making sure she didn't get detention was the best I could do.

I guess Betsy thought so too. When we were leaving for lunch, she said, "Albie?" really quiet.

"Yeah?" I said.

"Th-thanks," she told me.

I smiled, and Betsy smiled back. She held out her hand. Inside was a whole bag of gummy bears.

I'm not totally sure, but I think maybe me and Betsy are friends again.

lucky.

That night we all ate dinner at home, at the table, because Grandpa Park was visiting. It was real dinner too—steak and potatoes and even a salad with homemade dressing, not from a bottle or anything. Mom made it, and Dad set the table, which was usually my job. When I told Dad that, he said I could be in charge of loading the dishwasher instead, and that made me grouchy, because I hate loading the dishwasher. But I tried not to look grouchy in front of Grandpa Park. Grandpa Park doesn't like it when you're grouchy.

"So," Grandpa Park said after he bit into his steak. "Albie." He was talking with his mouth full, which I thought was something that was rude. But I guess when you're a grandpa, you can do whatever you want. I cut my own steak and tried not to look at the chewed-up food in his mouth. "How's Mountford?"

My eyeballs shot up from my plate. But Mom answered before I could say anything.

"Albie doesn't go to Mountford anymore, Appa," she told him. "You know that." Appa is what she calls Grandpa Park, because that's Korean for "Dad." I asked him once if I should call him *harabuji,* because that's what I thought Mom said the Korean word was for "grandfather." But Grandpa Park just swirled his glass with a clink of ice and said, "Not with that accent." So I stick to "grandpa."

"I most certainly did *not* know that," Grandpa Park said, stabbing at a piece of steak with his knife. He didn't even bother with the fork, just lifted the piece to his mouth and ate it right off the tip of the knife. "If I knew that, I wouldn't have asked about it. So." He turned to look straight at me, and I shifted my stare down to my salad, which suddenly I didn't want at all. "You're no longer going to the fancy private school your parents have been struggling so hard to pay for for the last six years. Why the hell not?"

Mom's eyes went big. "Appa!" she said.

But Grandpa Park kept staring at me. I could tell he was staring at me, even though I was still looking at my salad, not at him. I could feel his eyeballs boring into my brain.

"*Well?*" Grandpa Park said.

"Mom, next time can you put tomatoes in the salad?" I asked. "I really like tomatoes."

Mom put a hand on my arm. "Of course, honey," she said. "I'll be sure to remember."

Across the table, Dad set down his glass of wine. "We thought Albie would benefit more from going to a new school," he told Grandpa Park. "Mountford wasn't meeting his needs."

Grandpa Park snorted. "He got kicked out," he said. And the way he said it, it was like he knew it was a fact, like he knew it would happen all along, and he wasn't surprised at all. He maybe even thought it was sort of funny.

"I don't want to go to that stupid school anyway!" I said. Because I didn't. But then I slapped my hand over my mouth, because I was pretty sure I'd just yelled at Grandpa Park. And that was definitely something I was not supposed to do.

"Albie, sweetie," Mom said, her hand still on my arm, "why don't you go do your reading for your reading log?"

"I'm still eating," I told her.

"For your information," Dad told Grandpa Park—and he was glaring now, the kind of glaring I'd only seen him do when he was on the phone yelling at the cable guy—"P.S. 183 is an excellent school with a progressive philosophy on student—"

Grandpa Park snorted again. "A *public* school?" he said. "You're sending my grandson to a *public* school?"

"Albie," Mom said, squeezing my arm a little harder. Too hard. "Go do your reading." Her eyes were focused on my grandpa.

"Why bother?" Grandpa Park said. He pushed his plate aside and reached for his glass. He wasn't having wine like Mom and Dad. His glass was filled with the red-brown drink he always had when he visited, the one Mom kept up high in the cupboard just for him. "Why not just throw him in a ditch now and be done with it? That's where he'll end up at this rate."

"Appa!" Mom stood up then, her eyes angry-on-fire, and she practically pulled me out of my chair. "Come on, Albie. I think dinner's over."

"But . . . ," I said, because I'd only had two bites, and I was still hungry. But I didn't really want to stay either, so I followed her down the hall.

"Frankly," I heard my dad say as Mom dragged me away, "I don't appreciate the way you've been speaking to my son, Shin."

"Oh, really?" I heard Grandpa Park reply. "Because I don't appreciate the way you've been misraising my grandson."

That's when Mom slammed shut my bedroom door. She plopped herself down next to me on the bed and put her head in her hands.

I pulled the *Hatchet* book Mom gave me for my birthday

off the table next to my bed, and I held it out to her because I thought she wanted to help me with my reading, and that was why she came into my room. But she didn't take it. Instead she sighed.

I sighed too.

"I'm sorry about that, Albie," she said. She was looking at the closed door. The way she narrowed her eyes at it, you would've thought it was the door she was mad at.

"It's okay," I said. I didn't want her to feel bad. Anyway, it wasn't like I was upset or anything. I was pretty sure Grandpa Park was wrong about me ending up in a ditch.

"No," she said, still glaring at the door. "It's not."

I nodded. And I waited for her to tell me the stuff she usually told me when Grandpa Park came over, about him not really meaning all the stuff he said sometimes. And about him loving me so much, and that was why he could be so hard on me. And about him having a hard life growing up and so that was why he was gruff. Mom said the word *gruff* a lot when she was talking about Grandpa Park.

"Your grandfather . . ." She let out another long breath of air. "Your grandfather is not a very nice man."

I sort of laughed when she said that, because at first I thought she was joking. That definitely wasn't something you were supposed to say about your own dad. But when I looked at her face, I could tell she wasn't joking.

She closed her eyes and shook her head. "God, sometimes I could just. . ." She balled her hands up into little fists in her lap.

I hugged her then, around the side. I wasn't sure why I did it. Usually it was moms who hugged their kids, not the other way around. But I thought right then maybe she needed a hug more than I did.

She buried her nose deep in my hair. "I love you so much, Albie," she said softly.

Maybe my mom didn't always know how to be the best mother, like she said. But at least she was trying.

Maybe that was the important thing.

"I love you too," I told her. "You are caring and thoughtful and good."

Mom pulled away to look at me. Her eyes were wet. She smiled at me as she pushed the hair off my forehead, just gazing at my face. When she spoke, her voice was soft.

"Sometimes I wonder how I ever got so lucky to get a son like you, Albie."

Lucky.

That's what she said.

I hugged her again, around the side.

Maybe it was silly to not be upset at all when I could still hear my dad and Grandpa Park shouting at each other in the dining room. Maybe I should've been. But I wasn't.

Right then, I felt pretty lucky too.

being famous.

I wish I was famous," I told Erlan. We were sitting in his new bedroom, which was smaller than his bedroom at his old apartment, but at least it was only his bedroom, no brothers. Plus, Erlan had put the quilt up in front of his door, so he said the entire room was a quilt fort now, which meant no cameras ever.

"No, you don't," Erlan said. He was setting up the cards for our card game. The one called Spit, which Calista taught me. I was pretty good at that one, better than Erlan even, because you didn't have to count or anything, it was all about being fast. But it took forever to set it up every time, that was the only problem. Erlan was better at that part than I was.

"Yes, I do," I said. If I was famous, maybe I could have a bigger apartment too, like Erlan's family did. Maybe my family could have a billboard even, like the Kasteevs, with our faces on it, smiling happy. Maybe I could have all the toys I wanted, and everyone would like me and be friendly and nice to me, and my dad could quit his job, like Erlan's did, and just be home all the time with the family.

"No," Erlan said again. "You *don't*. Oh, man, I lost track. Now I have to start again." He scooped up all the cards.

Erlan was a smart kid, I knew that. You didn't get all *Excellent*s on your report card every year, and win the chess championships too, without being really smart. I *knew* that. But sometimes he could be dumb. "You don't even know what's good," I told him. And for some reason, I wasn't sure why, I said it really angry.

I *felt* angry.

Erlan's head shot up at me.

"You complain all the time," I told him, the angry still in my voice. "But what's so bad about being famous? You're on *TV*. That's so great!"

If I was on TV, instead of "no release!" Darren wouldn't make fun of me whispering behind his hand all the time. He wouldn't smash his finger into all my birthday cupcakes.

Erlan rolled his eyes. "You want to know what's so great

about being on TV?" he said to me. He wasn't setting up the game. He stopped. I wanted to tell him that he should start again, but I didn't. I waited. "Nothing. That's what. No one at school will even talk to me anymore. Everything that happens on that stupid show, they laugh about it all week. Even if Erik was the one who screamed like a girl when he saw that mouse, and everyone at school made fun of *me* for it. Erik pretends to be sick like every day so he doesn't have to go to school, and Karim just acts like a jerk, like he's so important. And Roza and Ainyr and Alma, they . . . It doesn't matter. I don't even care."

"Oh," I said. "I never even knew all that." I stared at the piles of cards. "How come you never told me before?"

Erlan shrugged. He scooped the piles together and started over setting them up. One, one. Five, five. Seven, seven. He counted out thirteen for the big piles. "You're the only one who treats me normal."

When the piles were all set up and it was time to start playing again, I picked up my pile of five, and at the same exact time, Erlan and I flipped over the one piles. And we were *off.*

Being famous maybe *sounded* like it would be fun, I thought, before you knew what it was really like. But it turned out it really wasn't at all.

Being famous sounded a whole lot like being cool.

a green
pencil.

Calista left a pencil at our house. A green one with no eraser, the kind she used for doing sketches in her sketchbook. When I found it, it made me sad in my stomach but happy too. I knew Calista couldn't take me to the park anymore or pick me up from school. She'd never take me for a donut day again.

But I had her pencil.

I found a fresh piece of paper in my drawer, and I smoothed it out against the top of the desk. Then I curled my fingers around that green pencil, and I started to draw.

Donut Man to the Rescue!

That's what I wrote at the top, when I was done with the drawing.

I was pretty sure Calista would have liked it.

studying
with betsy.

Studying for spelling tests with Betsy was different from studying with Calista. Usually, we went to her apartment after school, and her mom gave us cookies, the vanilla sandwich kind with chocolate in the middle. I always twisted mine open and ate the chocolate off first, one lick at a time. Betsy nibbled the whole cookie in circles, all the way around slowly, till she got to the final bite in the center.

We didn't make flash cards or draw pictures.

What we did was practice the spelling words, over and over and over. Betsy's mom read them out, and we took turns trying to spell them. I did mine out loud, and Betsy wrote hers on paper. If we got five or more right, we got another cookie. That's why I had to eat mine so slowly, with the licking. But I was starting to get more cookies.

I missed Calista a lot, but it wasn't so bad, studying with Betsy.

a famous schaffhauser grilled cheese.

H ow did the elections go this week?" Dad asked me. It was just me and him, since he was working from home after Harriet said she was done watching me and my parents should find a real nanny already. I was pretending to do social studies homework while Dad worked on his laptop. Really, I was doodling superheroes.

"Um," I said. Elections were a while ago, but I was surprised Dad remembered at all. "I ran for vice president," I told him. "But I lost." I clenched my stomach in a knot, waiting for all the disappointment.

"Oh," Dad said. "Well, that's all right, Albie. You can't win them all."

I unclenched my stomach just the tiniest bit. "Really?" I said.

"Sure." Dad clicked at his keyboard. "Only one person gets to be vice president, right? If there are a lot of people running, then you can't take it too much to heart if you don't get it."

"It was just one other person," I told him.

I don't know why I said that, really. I should've just let Dad be not disappointed in me, and not said anything at all. It was nice when Dad was not disappointed in me. But I guess I wanted him to be not disappointed in *me*, and not some made-up Albie who did really great in school elections.

Dad looked up from his laptop and frowned. "I bet you got a lot of votes, though," he said.

"Nope," I told him.

I was feeling like a pretty disappointing person.

But my dad surprised me. Because he pushed back his laptop on the table and said, "Did you want to be vice president very badly, Albie?" And he looked like he really wanted to know.

So I thought about it. "Yeah," I said at last. "At first I didn't, but"—I twirled my pencil in my fingers—"then it seemed like it would be fun. It would've been nice to win something."

Dad shut his laptop.

"Did I ever show you how to make a famous Schaff-hauser grilled cheese?" That's what he asked me.

Which seemed like a weird thing to ask.

I shook my head.

It turned out that the famous Schaffhauser grilled cheese was a grilled cheese sandwich that my dad learned how to make from *his* dad and that he said he wanted to teach me to make too.

The famous Schaffhauser grilled cheese was made with sourdough bread, not regular white.

The famous Schaffhauser grilled cheese had three differ-ent kinds of cheese in it—Swiss cheese and two other ones with funny-sounding names I couldn't pronounce. We had to walk six whole blocks in the snow to the fancy grocery store to get them all, which you'd think wouldn't be worth it, but Dad said it would be.

The famous Schaffhauser grilled cheese had a secret layer of Dijon mustard.

The famous Schaffhauser grilled cheese had to be made very precisely. First you put all the bread and the mustard and the cheese together. Not too much mustard.

Then you heated up the pan on the stove to exactly the right temperature, without anything even inside it. That part was important.

Then, while you were waiting for the pan to heat up, you spread butter on the outside sides of the sourdough bread. That was important too. Some people thought you melted the butter in the pan first to make grilled cheese, *then* put the sandwich down, but that was wrong because then the butter wouldn't spread even on the bread.

After that you had to stand and wait, patient patient patient, until you heard the Schaffhauser sizzle. That's how you knew to flip the sandwich over. I did it perfectly, exactly right. Dad said I was a natural.

The famous Schaffhauser grilled cheese was the best sandwich I ever ate.

"Can I ask you something, Albie?" Dad said while we chewed. "About the election?"

I looked at my famous Schaffhauser grilled cheese and found the perfect spot to take my next bite. "Sure," I said.

"Did you really want to be vice president?" Dad asked. "Or did you just want to win?"

I thought about that. Back before the elections, I would've said I wanted to be vice president more than anything. But really, who wanted to turn the classroom lights off?

"Maybe just winning," I said.

Dad nodded when I said that. "I think the hard thing for you, Albie," he told me, wiping his fingers off on a napkin, "is not going to be getting what you want in life, but figuring out what that is. Once you know what you want—really, truly—I know you'll get it."

I looked up at Dad while he took another bite of his

famous Schaffhauser grilled cheese. There was a funny thing about Dad, I thought. Because sometimes he didn't understand me at all. And sometimes, he understood me more than anyone else.

"Thanks," I said. And I took another bite of my own.

new lunch.

I stopped sitting at the lunch table with Darren and Candace and Lizzy and everyone. And reading *Captain Underpants* on the bench by myself. Now me and Betsy and Darissa ate our lunch in Mr. Clifton's room, which Mr. Clifton said was okay, even though Betsy wasn't actually in math club.

"We want to eat in here because we're not cool," I told him. Darissa wasn't cool either. She told me that right away, I think because she could tell I was worried she might be. But she didn't seem too upset about it. Darissa was friendly and funny and weird. She even knew how to do the Vulcan salute. She knew more about TV than any girl I'd ever met.

"Not being cool is cool with me," Mr. Clifton said. And after that he let us eat in there every day while he worked on lesson plans. The only rule was that we had to listen to one of his math jokes, which meant that I had to sit through two different ones every single day, which sometimes could be tough.

"Why didn't the quarter roll down the hill with the nickel?" That was the joke he told us on Tuesday.

"Because it had more cents!" That was the answer.

Betsy laughed at that one. She laughed at pretty much all of them.

After we were done eating, the three of us usually went outside to the blacktop. Darissa taught us a new handball game called Butt's Up, which none of us were very good at, but we liked playing because it had the word *butt* in it. And while we played, me and Betsy would tell her New York things she needed to know. Well, mostly me, but Betsy helped a little.

"The carriages with the horses are in Central Park," I told her. "But those aren't too much fun because the horse always poops a lot, and it smells *bad*." Betsy nodded to agree with me. "The better thing to do is to see the penguins in the Central Park Zoo, because they have a moving sidewalk in front of them, and the window steams up real good, so you can draw pictures on the windows for the penguins to see." I didn't tell her about the Bronx Zoo, and the python and the pig. I wasn't sure why, but I wanted to keep that one to myself.

Betsy nodded again. "You can wr-write n-notes on the w-window too," she said.

"Maybe we could go this weekend," Darissa said. "I'll have my dads ask your parents."

"Cool!" I said.

"Cool," Betsy said.

"And maybe we could ask my friend Erlan to come?" I asked.

"Is that the one who likes *Star Trek*?" Darissa wondered.

I told her he sure was, and Darissa gave the Vulcan salute. I was pretty sure that meant yes.

wednesday.

On Wednesday, Mr. Clifton told the best joke of all.

"Where's the best place in New York to learn multiplication?" he said.

And you wouldn't believe it, but I raised my hand. I'd never heard that joke before, but somehow, I don't know why, I knew the answer. It just popped into my head. So I raised my hand, good and high in the air.

"Albie?" Mr. Clifton said, calling on me.

Everyone turned to look at me then. No one hardly ever guessed the joke, except when it was a super-easy one we all knew anyway, like "seven ate nine." I was starting to get real nervous, like maybe I only *thought* I knew the answer but really I was wrong. But I answered anyway, just in case.

"Times Square?" I said.

And when everyone laughed and Mr. Clifton smiled huge, well, I knew I'd been right.

"That's a good one!" Jacob hooted.

Mr. Clifton gave me a gold star sticker. Me! A gold star sticker! I wore it all day on my sweatshirt. And when Darren Ackleman saw it and wrinkled up his nose and said, "What, do you think you're special or something?" I just told him, "Yep," and walked right on down the hallway.

gummy
bears.

On Monday we got our spelling tests back, and I got eight right, more than I'd ever gotten. That was a B. Which I figured I should've felt pretty happy about, because a B was better than a C or even a D, which was what I used to get on spelling tests. And I figured I should probably be pretty proud of myself too, because Betsy and I had studied really hard, and I knew that was why I did so well—the studying.

But actually I wasn't as happy as I probably should've been. Or as proud either. Because maybe it was silly, but I guess I thought just once I would get an A. And I guess maybe I thought it would happen that time.

I wondered what getting an A would feel like. The best feeling in the world, probably. Like going to a Yankees game with your dad and eating three hot dogs with extra everything.

But I didn't get an A. I got a B. Getting a B didn't feel like the best feeling in the world. It felt *almost* good. *Almost* happy. *Almost* proud. But not as good as an A.

I guess Betsy could tell I was feeling a little bit sad about the B, because when I was up at the front of the room sharpening my pencil, Betsy turned over the paper on my desk so you could see the grade, and right after the spot where Mrs. Rouse had written the B with her big red marker, Betsy wrote two other words, so that it said

B is for

And then after the *for,* Betsy had placed a gummy bear, right at the top of the test. A red one.

"B is for Bear," I said, reading. And I popped the gummy bear in my mouth. Betsy smiled at me, and right then, I felt really glad about getting a B. I could tell Betsy was proud of me.

"You should get a gummy bear too," I told her, looking at her test. "You should get a bunch, since you got an A." An A was way better than a B, so it only made sense that you would get more gummy bears for that.

Betsy shook her head, and before I could ask her why,

Mrs. Rouse shushed us for talking during silent reading, so she wouldn't've been able to talk anyway. Instead she wrote a note on the corner of her notebook, and twisted it so I could see.

A isn't for Bear. That's what the note said. *Only B is.*

I thought about that, and then I wrote a note on the corner of my own notebook.

What's A for?

That's what my note said. Usually I always thought *A* was for Albie, but that didn't make sense this time.

Betsy just shrugged, and when Mrs. Rouse got up to get something from the closet, Betsy wrote me a new note.

Anchovies?

It took me a long time to sound out the word, but when I finally did, when I figured out that Betsy meant those tiny smelly fish that no one *ever* wants on pizza, I laughed so hard I almost got both of us in trouble again.

If *A* was for anchovies, then I was glad I got a *B.*

I thought about it a lot that whole afternoon, and finally I decided that I didn't think *A* was for anchovies after all. I worked really hard on my plan all night, and the next morning I gave Betsy the card.

A is for Art!

That's what it said on the front. And on the inside, it was full of all the best drawings that Calista had taught me how to do—superheroes and unicorns and donuts and all my favorite stuff to draw. It said *Good job, Betsy!* in huge blue letters.

I could tell that Betsy liked it, because she tucked it carefully into her folder, and then she looked up at me and said, "Thanks, Albie." And Betsy only said something when she really meant it.

smoothing
out the edges.

After a while, Darren Ackleman mostly ignored me completely, like he didn't know I was alive at all. Not all days. But most days.

Some days, he pushed his shoulder into me while I was getting into my cubby.

Some days, he called me "dummy" or "retard" or worse.

Some days, it bothered me.

Some days, it didn't.

But every day, what I tried to do was to roll the names

Darren called me around in my head, over over over, until the edges were smooth and the words weren't so painful.

Sometimes it worked.

Sometimes it didn't.

But still I kept rolling. That was the only thing I had to do.

superpowers.

I hadn't been to visit Hugo in a long time, because I guess I just wasn't feeling that much like donuts, but Monday after school I decided to go. I told my new baby-sitter, Nadine, that I wanted to go downstairs to get a snack and that Mom always let me go by myself, and after I said that, she let me go right down the elevator and right out the front door of the building, even though what I'd said about Mom letting me go by myself was a lie.

I figured out that maybe Nadine was not a very good babysitter.

Hugo was super happy to see me. He finished scooping sugar into a customer's coffee cup and waved at me. "Albie!" he said when I walked through the door. "What's new?"

"I got two B's in a row on my spelling tests," I told him.

"Albie!" he said. "That's great. You've been really studying, huh?"

I shrugged. Then I got to picking out a donut. Hugo didn't say anything else, just went back to straightening things behind the counter.

But then he did say something.

"You know, Calista was here the other day." That's what he said.

My head shot up. "She was?" My heart felt like it was racing just a little bit in my chest. "Did she say anything?"

Hugo straightened a box of gum packs on the counter. "She said to say hi when I saw you," he told me. "So, hi."

"Hi," I answered. I felt a little bit sunken-in, in my chest, all of a sudden. I wished I could've told Calista about my B's in spelling. She'd be real excited for me, I knew it. "I wish she'd come to see *me*," I said. But even right when I said it, I knew she couldn't. I knew she couldn't come up to my apartment to see me for the same reason I couldn't call her on the phone anymore, even if I wanted to all the time. Because she wasn't my babysitter anymore, and my mom would be mad. And it wasn't fair to Calista to have people be mad at her, even if it was people who were only trying their best to be good moms.

"I've missed you around here, you know," Hugo said.

"You have?" I asked. I thought Hugo only liked talking to Calista.

Hugo nodded. "Course I did. Plus, I've got coffee cups up to my eyeballs." Hugo swept his arm toward the corner where, sure enough, the tower of coffee cups was teetering like it was about to topple. But it wasn't quite up to his eyeballs. I think he was exaggerating about that.

"I guess I better get to work, then," I said.

"I guess you better."

I headed over to the coffee corner.

"Albie?" Hugo said. I looked back. "Calista asked if she could check the stock when she was here, and she said she thought there might be something wrong with the newest shipment of coffee sleeves."

"Something wrong?"

Hugo shrugged. "I don't know. But if I were you, I'd look in the back." He pointed. "The stack closest to the door, I believe."

The first thing I noticed about the pack of coffee sleeves by the door was that the plastic was already open. That was weird.

What was weirder, though, was that two sleeves from the top, when I pulled them out to check, there was a picture. In thin black marker, right on the sleeve, someone had drawn a picture. And I thought I knew who.

Underneath it was another coffee sleeve, with another picture.

Then another one, right under that.

On the next one, the picture of Donut Man looked just how I felt.

And then there was another coffee sleeve with a picture of Art Girl, and then under that, four with mostly just words.

．． ．

When Nadine came down to the bodega thirty minutes later, she was mad, because she said she thought I'd run off and been hit by a bus or something, and also she talked to my mom who said that no way was I allowed to leave the apartment by myself, so boy, was I in trouble. But I didn't mind. That's because I had a secret.

Under the sleeves of my sweatshirt, I had two cuffs around my wrists, just like the superheroes sometimes wore in the comics. One had a drawing of a donut on it. And the other one said KIND.

And for the first time in maybe forever, I really did feel like I might just have superpowers.

almost.

I took that *B is for Bear* spelling test from a couple weeks
before, and I taped it to my door, right underneath my
letter from Mountford. I knew what Dad would probably
say if he saw it, that even if a B was almost an A, that almost wasn't good enough.

But I knew something else too.

You couldn't get where you were going without knowing
where you'd been.

And you couldn't be anywhere at all without having been
almost there for a while.

things i know.

I know the quickest way from JFK to 59th and Park in a cab, and I can tell the driver too.

I know all the best dog parks in Manhattan to go look at dogs, and all the best playgrounds, and which avenues go south and which go north and which ones go both ways.

I know how to put the key in the lock in our front door nearly-all-the-way-in-but-not-quite, so it won't stick.

I know how to slice an apple with only four cuts, so there's no core, only fruit.

I know that Erlan could beat me at Spit if he really

wanted to, because he can be fast as lightning. But I know he never will, because he doesn't mind when I win (and I don't mind it either).

I know that when Betsy bites her lip, she's nervous. I know that when she jiggles her left foot in class, she knows the answer but doesn't want to raise her hand. I know that Betsy knows a lot more than she says.

I know that sometimes math isn't as terrible as you might think, especially if it has to do with cup stacking. Or joke telling.

I know that parents don't always know exactly what they're doing, even if they're trying their hardest.

I know that even cool kids wish they weren't cool sometimes.

I know, at least I think I do, maybe, sometimes, definitely, what I'm worth.

I know what I'm worth.

I absolutely almost do.

There are a lot of things I know.

Turn the page for a sample of
LISA GRAFF's magical novel

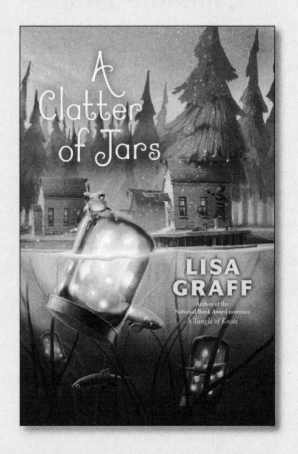

Companion to the
National Book Award nominee
A TANGLE OF KNOTS

Lily's Watermelon Limeade Float

— a drink reminiscent of all the best birthday parties —

FOR THE WATERMELON LIMEADE:
  4 cups chopped watermelon, from half of one small
    watermelon
  2 tbsp lime juice, from one lime
  1/2 cup sugar
  1 liter (4 cups) seltzer

FOR THE FLOAT:
  vanilla ice cream

1. In a blender or food processor, blend the watermelon, lime
   juice, sugar, and seltzer for just a few seconds, until smooth.
   Carefully pour through a wire-mesh strainer into a 2-quart
   pitcher. Discard the solids.

2. To serve, scoop ice cream into the bottom of a short glass.
   Pour the watermelon limeade over the top, and enjoy!

   [Serves 8]

Lily

LILY STOOD OUTSIDE THE DOOR TO THE INFIRMARY, winding the length of swampy green yarn around her right thumb. In every corner of the woods, campers were squealing, laughing, making friends, and generally kicking up a lot of dust. But Lily was focused on that length of yarn.

"Liliana Vera?"

In front of Lily stood a lanky counselor wearing a pine green Camp Atropos T-shirt, the name *Del* printed below the neckline.

"Are you Liliana?" Del asked. "I'm gathering Cabin Eight campers."

Lily glanced past Del to the flag circle, where four campers stood amid their luggage. "I'm Lily," she said.

"Great!" Del jerked his chin toward her duffel bag. "Need help with that?"

Lily shook her head, her wavy brown hair grazing her shoulders. "I got it," she said. Del looked skeptical, probably because Lily was hardly taller than the duffel was long. But Lily focused her thoughts at the bridge of her nose and, darting her eyes to the duffel, the bag rose—one inch, then five—off the ground. Lily took a step forward in the dirt, and the bag took a step with her.

"No need to ask what *your* Talent is," Del said, watching the bag drift forward. "Been a while since we had a Pinnacle here." Lily swelled with the smallest inkling of pride. "Welcome to Camp Atropos for Singular Talents, Liliana Vera. A haven for the most remarkable children in the world." As they neared the flag circle, Del pointed to each of the four campers, rattling off names. "Miles, Renny, Chuck, and Ellie." Lily did a double take when Del named the last two. Chuck and Ellie were identical twin girls. "Your bunkmates for the next two weeks. Let's get you all to Cabin Eight, shall we?"

"Hi!" Ellie greeted Lily as they began their trek though the woods. Lily could tell the twins apart because, despite having identical faces and identical dark brown skin, Ellie had a headful of teeny braids pulled into a ponytail and was wearing pale blue sneakers, while Chuck's hair was styled into wavy cornrows, and she wore Kelly-green high-tops. "Do you like frogs?" Ellie asked. "Chuck and I can identify any species."

"Uh," Lily replied. "Cool."

That's when one of the boys, Miles, piped up. "Singular Talents are understood as feats beyond standard human abilities and/or the laws of physics," he said. His voice was flat, his gaze fixed on the dirt in front of him as he walked.

"Huh?" Ellie asked.

"I think what he means," said the other boy, Renny, "is that identifying frogs isn't a Singular Talent. Either that or he just likes showing off how much of that textbook he memorized."

Beside her sister, Chuck snorted. "Oh, man," she said. "They're on to us now, Ellie. I guess we'll have to leave and go to regular person camp."

Ellie poked her twin in the side. "Chuck, *please*," she said.

They were deep in the shadows of the trees when Renny joined step beside Lily. He was tall and skinny, with pasty white legs. "Is this your brother?" Renny asked, his nose buried in a small photo book. He flipped a page. "Cute kid."

"Hey!" Lily cried, realizing what Renny was holding. "Give me that!" Focusing her thoughts at the bridge of her nose, she tugged the photo book toward her through the air. With her concentration no longer upon it, her duffel thunked to the dirt. The front pocket had been zipped open.

Lily inspected the album for damage, wiping away a smudge from the photo of Max's fifth birthday party three years earlier. It was one of Lily's favorites. Her little brother was balancing a plate of chocolate cake on his pinkie, his other arm wrapped around Lily. Lily, meanwhile, was using her own Talent to push the cake toward Max's nose. It was the last birthday she and Max had celebrated before their mother remarried and their step-sister, Hannah, buzzed into their lives like a housefly. Hannah had to go and be born the same day as Max—same year and everything—so in every birthday photo after that, it was Hannah that Max had his arm around.

At least Hannah had been assigned to a different cabin for the two weeks of camp, Lily reminded herself, zipping the photo book back in its pocket. She hoisted the duffel to her shoulder, which immediately ached in protest.

"You should keep a better eye on your stuff," Renny said. And when Lily scowled, he didn't even have the decency to look sorry. Instead, he stretched out his arm, like he wanted to shake hands. "Renwick Fennelbridge," he told her. "You might have heard of me."

Despite herself, Lily was impressed. She'd studied the Fennelbridges last year in her Singular Education elective, and she found them fascinating. Every family member was Singular, with some of the most fantastical Talents ever recorded.

"Can you really read minds?" she asked.

That's when the other boy, Miles, piped up again. "Renwick Chester Ulysses Fennelbridge," he said, his eyes still fixed on the dirt. "Eleven years old as of his last birthday. The only living Scanner, according to *A Singular History*. Fun fact: Renwick Fennelbridge was once flown to Rome, Italy, to read the mind of the pope, but got food poisoning on the plane and had to go home."

"*Please* find a new fun fact, Miles," Renny grumbled.

"You really know your Talent history, huh?" Lily said to Miles. Singular Education had been Lily's favorite class last year. Her teacher had been so impressed with her report on Ekers and Coaxes that she'd had Lily read it during the opening ceremony of the Talent festival. "Do you know about Evrim Boz?"

Miles responded without hesitation. "Evrim Biber Boz. Born 1576, died 1602. Talent: Coax. Able to wheedle Talents from one person to another and back again, even transferring Talents into inanimate objects to create Artifacts. Fun fact: The Talent Library in Munich, Germany, has eight of Evrim Boz's Artifacts on display, including a cooking pot that makes anything boiled inside taste like lentil stew."

"Did you know that later in her life, Evrim Boz said she wished she'd never created any Artifacts at all?" Lily asked, scurrying to keep up with him. Unlike Ekers, who could only steal Talents, Coaxes could pass Talents on—either to other people or to objects. "Because once you make an Artifact, you can't get the Talent back out. Evrim Boz tried once, with a pair of scissors that she'd Coaxed a beard-trimming Talent into, and instead she accidentally replaced the beard-trimming with her brother's Talent for cartography." Lily had always had a particular interest in Artifacts and the people who used them. "Evrim Boz's brother never spoke to her after that."

Miles didn't even glance at Lily before continuing his recitation. "Maevis Marion Marvallous. Sixty-seven years old as of her last birthday. Talent: Mimic. Able to duplicate the Talent of any person she comes in contact with for approximately one year."

"Now you've set him off," Renny muttered. "When Miles gets started on Talent history, good luck getting him to stop."

"Fun fact," Miles went on. "Maevis Marvallous alleges that she lost her Talent over three decades ago, although scholars debate the claim."

Suddenly Lily noticed that Miles and Renny had the same sharp nose. Same auburn hair. Same pasty knees. Miles was a bit broader, but they were brothers, no question.

"I didn't know there were two Fennelbridge kids," Lily said. She was sure *A Singular History* had mentioned only one. "What's his Talent?"

Renny halted midstride to tug at the top of his right sock. "Make enough Fennelbridges, and one of them's bound to be Fair." He let out a sour laugh. "That's what our dad likes to say."

"If you ask me," Chuck chimed in, "there are two Fair kids in the Fennelbridge family."

"What do you mean by that?" Renny snapped.

"You obviously stink at reading minds," Chuck informed him. "I've been mentally threatening to pop you in the jaw for the past ten minutes, and you haven't flinched once."

Lily couldn't help it. She laughed.

Oblivious to the awkwardness behind him, Del pointed to a sturdy building hewn from logs. "There's the lodge," he called back. "Meals are served on the mess deck. All-camp slumber party's the second Friday of camp, and the Talent show's that Sunday, before your parents take you home."

At the mention of the Talent show, Lily's heart snagged her chest. Maybe there was still time to come up with a new act to perform with Max.

A lot could happen in two weeks.

"The lodge also houses the office of our camp director, Jo," Del continued. "She plays a mean harmonica."

Miles broke from his Talent history just long enough to tell the dirt, "I play a nice harmonica. I learned last year in music. Cassandra Colby Donovan. Born 1851, died 1900. Talent: Quest. Fun fact: Cassandra Donovan was the Needle-in-a-Haystack champion of Baxley, Georgia, for forty years running, until they retired the competition."

"Up ahead is the archery ring," Del went on. "There's the fire pit, where we hold our campfire each Friday. And if you squint, you can make out the lake through the trees."

At that, Miles stopped walking. "No water!" he squeaked.

Del offered Miles a friendly smile. "What's wrong with a little"—he spit into one hand and pressed his palms together before sprinkling miniature icicles in the dirt—"*water?*" He took in Miles's alarmed expression. "Not a fan of a classic Numbing Talent, huh?" Del cleared his throat. The ice-spit at his feet was already melting in the sun. "Uh . . . canoes are available every day after breakfast, and if you feel like swimming, Jo encourages you to grab your towel any time of day and hop right in the water."

"*No water!*"

Miles shrieked it that time. And he began flicking his fingers, too—*flick-flick-flick-flick-flick!*

Quick as lightning, Renny grabbed his brother's hand. "You guys sell Caramel Crème bars at the camp store, right?" Renny asked Del. Miles's fingers slowly ceased their flicking. "Miles loves Caramel Crème bars."

"I want a Caramel Crème bar," Miles said, pulling his hand free. If Lily hadn't witnessed the scene herself, she'd never have believed that Miles had been in a near panic thirty seconds earlier.

"Uh . . ." Del scratched a spot below his ear. "What was the question again?"

"Caramel Crème bars," Renny reminded him.

"Oh. Right."

As Del went over the store's hours, Lily wound the length of yarn around her thumb, watching Renny with his brother. Lily had tied the yarn around her thumb three weeks ago. Since then, the lime green strands had turned swampy, thinning and separating, and the skin underneath had grown raw from constant rubbing. It had stung for some time, like a blister—insistent, sharp, painful. But Lily hadn't untied it.

She tugged her duffel farther up her aching shoulder, her attention stolen by the music drifting through one of the lodge's windows. It was a song Lily was quite familiar with. This was an instrumental version, without lyrics, but Lily knew the words by heart.

Los golpes en la vida
preparan nuestros corazones
como el fuego forja al acero.

Lily and Max's father had sung them the melancholy lullaby countless times, on nights when he wasn't traveling for work. When he sang the tune, the notes swept you up and cradled you, made you feel safe.

("Why do you always have to travel?" Lily had asked him last year, when he'd been in Prague instead of her school auditorium for the opening ceremony of the Talent festival. He'd responded as he always did. Not that it was his job—not that he *had* to be away so often, that he had no choice—but rather: "Oh,

Liria. Traveling helps ease my heartache." Which didn't explain why her father had begun his travels long before he and Lily's mother had been married.)

Lily let the words of the song sink in. Her father had translated the lyrics for her once, but she never felt she truly understood them in any language.

> *The blows of life*
> *prepare our hearts*
> *like fire forges iron.*

Summer camp, Lily thought, pulling herself from the music to rejoin the tour, didn't seem like a place for melancholy songs.

When they reached Cabin Eight, Del creaked open the door and let them inside.

"Cordelia Fabius Sibson," Miles said as he entered the cabin. "Eighty-two years old as of her last birthday. Talent: Scribe."

Lily wound the length of yarn around her right thumb, staring at the three bunks that lined the cabin walls.

Three bunks.

Six beds.

"Are we waiting for another camper?" Chuck asked Del. "There are six beds, and only five of us."

"The assignments for this cabin were a little odd," Del

admitted. "I don't know what Jo was thinking, but you don't question Jo. Anyway, you were supposed to have one more cabinmate, but at the last minute, he—"

Lily dropped her duffel with a heavy *thunk*. "I need to go to the infirmary," she said.

"You okay?" Del asked, stitching his eyebrows together.

"I have to go," Lily repeated. And she squeezed past him out the door, racing down the path. Kicking up dirt.

It should have been Max in that sixth bed. It should have been their summer together, while Hannah the housefly was far off in a different cabin, buzzing at someone else. But they weren't together, because three weeks ago, Max had gotten hurt.

Around and around went the length of yarn.

Lily was the one who'd hurt him.

Keep reading to preview

LISA GRAFF's novel

We double dog dare you . . .

1.

A pair of boys' underwear

One.

Two.

Those were the numbers written on either side of the chalkboard in Miss Sparks's fourth-grade classroom on Thursday morning. Francine stared at them as she drummed her fingers on her desktop, waiting for Media Club to officially start. Waiting for Kansas to walk through the classroom door. He was taking *forever*.

One.

Two.

Francine had only been in this war with Kansas for two days, and already she was behind. She had one point, and Kansas had two. Yesterday, when she'd been dared to hang

13

upside down from the monkey bars for all of second recess, the blood had rushed to her head somewhere around the eleventh minute or so, and she'd gotten dizzy and suddenly found herself—*PLOP!*—facedown on the grass with a raging headache. Kansas had been able to do *his* dare, no problem— telling the yard monitor, Mr. DuPree, that he needed to smell his armpit for a science project—so he was ahead, two points to one. But did that mean he was more worthy of being the news anchor than Francine was? No, of course not.

Francine just had to prove it.

"Francine?" Natalie asked, nudging her in the side with her elbow. "You want some pudding?"

Francine looked over at her friend, who was sitting at the desk next to her. Natalie was holding out a pudding cup from her lunch bag.

"But it's not lunch yet," Francine said. Francine's mother was morally opposed to any food that tasted good, so Natalie always shared hers. Chocolate pudding days were especially exciting. "If I eat it now, all I'll have for lunch is fava bean salad."

"Take it," Natalie said, pushing the pudding cup closer

to Francine's nose. She dug a plastic spoon out of her lunch bag, too. "You look like you need it."

"Thanks," Francine replied, taking the pudding and the plastic spoon. She was particularly grateful for the spoon. Natalie's mom usually packed real silverware in her daughter's lunch, but when there was chocolate pudding, Natalie always tried to sneak in a plastic spoon for Francine. That's because Francine felt strongly that chocolate pudding tasted one thousand times more delicious with a plastic spoon, instead of a metal one. She couldn't understand why everyone didn't eat it that way.

Francine peeled the foil lid off the pudding cup and licked the underside. The chocolate melted on the outside edges of her tongue, smooth and creamy and perfect. Just what she needed. "I guess I am a little jumpy," she told Natalie. Her eyes drifted to the backpack on her desk, where she was keeping her secret weapon—the thing that was going to help her defeat Kansas Bloom for sure.

Only . . . what if it didn't?

"You're really going to do it?" Natalie asked, her eyes focused on Francine's backpack, too.

Francine gulped down a mouthful of pudding, and did her best to sound confident. "Yep," she said.

"Well"—Natalie crumpled her lunch bag closed, just as Kansas strolled through the door—"good luck." And she stood up and joined the other members at the clump of desks in the corner, where they were studying that morning's newspaper.

"Thanks," Francine said, scraping out the last dregs of chocolate pudding. But she knew that real winners didn't need luck. Real winners needed courage.

When she was sure that Miss Sparks was distracted on the other side of the room, searching through her desk drawer for something, Francine made her way over to the other members of the club. With his floppy hair and ruddy cheeks, Kansas was looking cool and calm, just like the King of Dares he thought he was. Well, Francine would show him. Not even the King of Dares would do what she had planned for him.

Taking a deep breath of courage, Francine plopped her backpack dead center on the group of desks.

"What's that?" Luis asked.

"That," Francine replied, allowing herself the smallest

of smiles, "is Kansas's new dare." And, while everyone watched, Francine slowly, tooth by tooth, tugged open the zipper of her backpack. Then, with the eraser end of a number-two pencil, Francine pulled out her secret weapon and raised it from her backpack for everyone to see.

A white pair of boys' underwear, slightly used.

Emma squealed. Luis's eyes went huge, his lips round as he whistled out a "nooooooo way!" Andre snorted and thumped Kansas square on the back. "Oh, man," he said, shaking his head. "Oh, *man*."

But Kansas was silent.

"Whose are they?" Brendan asked.

Francine paused a moment. If there was anyone in that room who should know whose tighty whities they were, it was Brendan King. After all, he'd been the one who swiped them from the boys' locker room during PE yesterday while Kansas was changing. Francine had paid him five bucks to do it. The whole dare had been his idea. But he was probably just trying to cover up so no one would suspect him of being an underwear thief.

Francine stood up a little straighter, swinging the briefs from her pencil like a pendulum. "See for yourselves," she told them. And she flung the underwear down in front of Kansas's perched elbows so that the name on the waistband was completely visible.

Kansas Bloom. The words were written in neat, square permanent marker.

Emma squealed again, so loudly that Miss Sparks popped her head up from behind her desk to see what was going on. Alicia had the sense to cover for them, fanning out the pages of the morning's newspaper and exclaiming loudly, "I cannot *believe* this thing about the strike in Greece!"

Miss Sparks went back to rummaging.

Luis inspected the briefs. "You write your name in your underwear?" he asked Kansas.

Kansas was doing his best to ignore the underwear just two inches from his left elbow. "No," he said, flicking his eyes up to meet Francine's, "I don't."

Brendan snorted. "Well, then I guess your mom does," he replied.

"What's the dare?" Alicia asked, scrunching the newspaper aside to get a closer look at the underwear.

This was it, Francine thought. This was the moment when Kansas would say, "Fine, I give up, you got me."

This was the moment when Francine would finally, officially, win the war and be declared the future news anchor of Media Club for spring semester. Just the way it should've been all along.

"I double dog dare you," she told Kansas, her stomach fluttering with the excitement of the moment. This must be how generals felt when they were about to defeat their enemies. "To string your underwear up the flagpole."

The members of the Media Club gasped. "Wow," Alicia said. "That's *good*."

"We need to vote on it," Luis reminded them, "before it's an official dare. All in favor?"

They were all in favor.

Francine turned to Kansas. She wanted to be sure to catch the exact moment when he threw his hands up in the air and quit.

But he didn't do that at all. Instead, as cool as ever, Kansas scooped his underwear off the table and said, "You want me to do it right now?"

"Wait," Francine said. "You mean you're actually going to *do* it?"

"Of course I'm going to do it," Kansas said, rolling his

eyes. Like Francine's dare was nothing to him. Like *she* was nothing. "I told you, I've never turned down a dare in my life. I'm the King of Dares."

Then he slid his chair back, the feet making an awful *thrummmmm* against the linoleum, stuffed the briefs into his back pocket, and walked across the classroom. On the way, he gave Francine a little shove, right in the shoulder. It might have been an accident. But Francine knew it wasn't.

"I can't believe he's going to do it," Natalie whispered under her breath, after the door had shut behind him. "He's so *brave*." Francine frowned at her. "Oh. But, I mean, you're totally going to win, though. Obviously." She offered her elbow to Francine, who took it after only a second's pause, and together they joined the other club members at the window, where they were already swarming for the best view of the flagpole.

The magic of *Savvy* meets
the complexity of *When You Reach Me*
in this "blithe magical puzzle."
—*The Wall Street Journal*

A National Book Award Nominee!

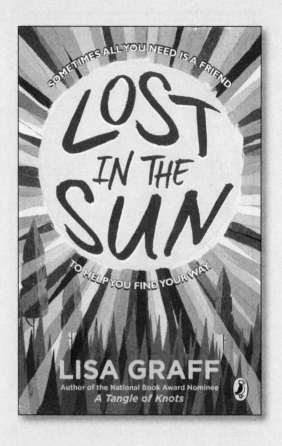

SOMETIMES ALL YOU NEED IS A FRIEND

LOST IN THE SUN

TO HELP YOU FIND YOUR WAY.

LISA GRAFF

Author of the National Book Award Nominee
A Tangle of Knots

Trent caused the accident that killed one of his teammates. And all he did was shoot a hockey puck. Middle school could be the chance at a fresh start. Maybe he'll blend in. Maybe all will be forgotten. Maybe he can even join the baseball team. But none of that seems likely. Then he meets Fallon Little—the girl with the mysterious scar across her face—and starts to realize that everyone has their secrets, and it might just be possible, after all, to start over.

LISA GRAFF

Author of the National Book Award Nominee
A Tangle of Knots

IT'LL TAKE MORE THAN
A FEW MAGIC TRICKS
TO GET HER
OUT OF THIS MESS

THE LIFE
AND CRIMES OF
BERNETTA
WALLFLOWER

Bernetta's summer couldn't be going any worse. First her ex-best friend frames her for starting a cheating ring in their private school that causes Bernetta to lose her scholarship for seventh grade. Even worse, Bernetta's parents don't believe she's innocent and forbid her from performing at her father's magic club. Now Bernetta must take immediate action if she hopes to raise $9,000 for tuition. But that's a near impossible task with only three months until school. Enter Gabe, a boy con artist who's willing to team up with Bernetta to raise the money. But only if she's willing to use her talent for magic to scheme her way to success.